A Case for Christianity

A Case
for
Christianity

MORRIS A. INCH, PH.D.

Tyndale House Publishers, Inc.
WHEATON, ILLINOIS

Library of Congress Cataloging-in-Publication data

Inch, Morris A., date
  A case for Christianity / Morris A. Inch.
    p.   cm.
  Includes bibliographical references (p.   ).
  ISBN 0-8423-0325-1 (sc : alk. paper)
  1. Apologetics.   I. Title
BT1102.I55   1997
239—dc21   96-51503

Printed in the United States of America

03   02   01   00   99   98   97
 7   6   5   4   3   2   1

239
I

CONTENTS

PREFACE

"You must worship Christ as Lord of your life. And if you are asked about your Christian hope, always be ready to explain it. But you must do this in a gentle and respectful way" (1 Peter 3:15-16), wrote the apostle Peter in his first-century address to believers scattered throughout Asia Minor. Peter's challenge to the early Christians is just as relevant for believers proclaiming the gospel today, for twenty centuries later we still find ourselves scattered in a hostile world. The task remains the same. From Peter's call, translated here as "explain," and in some other versions as a "defense," we derive the term *apologetics*. Apologetics is a reasoned response to why we believe as we do.

Apologetics is not something which we should leave to the spur of the moment. It requires careful preparation. Nor should it be delegated to ministry professionals, for it is the responsibility of all. It is not an option, but a biblical mandate. Our God deserves to have his gospel and his glory defended in ways that bring honor to him.

Even so, I have repeatedly been asked the question: "Why should I be concerned with apologetics?" Simply put, if you are a Christian, God requires it. He admonishes us to be prepared with a rationale for our faith. He does not simply invite us, but commands our involvement. No other reason or combination of reasons would prove a greater incentive.

This is not to imply that there are no attending reasons. Quite the reverse! For one thing, apologetics serves to bolster our confidence. It suggests that we have nothing to fear but fear itself.

It also contributes to our ministry. Some people raise legitimate questions that we can, if properly prepared, assist them in answering. We can't impose faith on others, but we can break up the ground for it to take root and grow.

What if a person is not a Christian? Has he or she any reason to delve into apologetics? Yes, indeed! Any serious-minded person should be interested in the rationale for the Christian faith, since no alternative religion or philosophy has impacted so many so profoundly in the course of history. Such evidence should compel us all to further investigate the matter.

You may well ask: "Why read this book in particular?" There are certainly other apologetics books which cover the subject in more detail and excel in one regard or another.

While no two apologetic works are alike, this is more distinctive than most. The topics range broadly to incorporate more traditional concerns along with contemporary issues growing out of the experiences of Christians living with cross-cultural awareness.

I take a simple, but hopefully not simplistic, approach to the topic. Having taught apologetics over the years, I am well aware that the issues could be treated in much more depth. However, profound truths can usually be expressed simply. We ought not to confuse profundity with obscurity.

Do I exclude the more informed apologetic reader as a result? Certainly not! Those better versed in apologetics should discover profitable insights, if not for themselves then to assist those to whom they minister. As a rule, one ought always to read with others in mind.

No doubt a full and rich life has contributed much to this small volume. I seldom attended church as a youth, and looked on the Christian faith as an outsider. It was not until serving in the military during World War II that I became a disciple of Christ. Both my early experience and conversion have left a lasting impression on which to draw for apologetic purposes.

My years of study cultivated what D. Elton Trueblood refers to as "disciplined insight," which he concluded is necessary to earn a hearing. I suppose there are some who, if for no other reason, would be interested in why a rather educated person might believe. They might discover in so doing that what they had previously rejected as untenable was, in fact, a less-informed and immature version of Christian faith.

No one learns more than the instructor, or so it would seem in my case. I have benefited from some very keen students. Together, we have probed the sometimes subtle rationale for faith. They have contributed indirectly to this present volume and its value to the reader.

It is in connection with cross-cultural experience that my apologetic perspective has taken final shape. Time spent in Greece, Romania, Israel, Japan, Korea, Taiwan, Singapore, Hong Kong, and Malaysia has been invaluable in creating a more cosmopolitan apologetic. Hence, it would appear more beneficial for the modern North American reader and more adaptable for others.

The preceding considerations seem to suggest a wide reading audience for this particular text. I imagine it being read by a businessman riding the commuter train, a young mother interested in sharing the claims of Christ with a neighbor, or a student learning more about his or her faith. It is also something one might share with a friend who is seriously searching for the illusive meaning of life.

The order of topics ranges from philosophic apologetics to Christian evidences, interwoven in a distinctive fashion to provide better cohesion. The case builds from theistic apologetics in general to Christian apologetics in particular. It reaches its eventual climax with the pointed question: "Is Christianity credible?"

Finally, I wish to extend special appreciation to my cherished wife, Joan, not only for her contribution in preparing the manuscript but for her unfailing encouragement, and to Robert Hosack and David Barrett for their helpful suggestions.

INTRODUCTION: WADING IN

Where are we going? What do we hope to find? When shall we know that we have succeeded?

Such questions remind me of my childhood swimming experiences. The water always seemed a bit threatening. While never wanting to get in over my head, I realized that it would be necessary to wade in far enough to refine my sorely limited aquatic skills.

So it is with our discussion of Christian apologetics. We must approach our topic seriously, but without attempting to do too much too soon. We will not be diving in; rather, we will wade in slowly. Should the water appear inviting, you may want to consider apologetics in more detail.

WHERE WE ARE GOING

First of all, where are we going? That's simple—to inquire into why Christians believe as they do. Others have delved into this topic before, as we shall see from two early chapters on the history of Christian apologetics. We are in their debt.

Before returning to the past, we shall look at the contextual question: "What is truth?" (The Christian faith is not what we wish were true, but believe to be true.) We will consider various criteria for determining truth, nudging ever closer to Jesus' astonishing claim to embody truth.

We will also look at the reported experience of God as a distinctive truth claim. While not an altogether conclusive criterion, it deserves special consideration.

After our historical reflection, we will delve into the traditional arguments for belief in God and the credibility issue created by suffering. These chapters constitute an abbreviated case for theism—belief in a personal God.

In the process we will come to realize that we as humans experience faith in common, which allows us to view life as a meaningful whole. Our alternatives are not between faith and its absence, but credible faith and credulity (an undue readiness to believe). With such in mind, we consider the reasons people have given for believing in God's existence, reflecting on both their merit and limitations.

Suffering proves not to be an insurmountable problem for faith, Christian or otherwise. The "answer" to suffering lies more with living than abstract reasoning, and so we introduce the "theodicies" (defenses of God's power and goodness in view of evil) of Job and Jesus. In particular, this accents what C. S. Lewis refers to as "complex good," God's providential care extended in a fallen world of spiritual conflict. For me, life resembles experiences in the military during wartime, when suffering proves indiscriminate, and the quest for God seems especially urgent.

We will next focus our attention on humankind, created in God's image as steward of his larger creation but now also fallen and in need of redemption. Here we sense that our experience fits well with the biblical account.

Appropriate to the above, we take up the prospect of immortality. First in general terms and then in regard to the resurrection of Jesus and its implications for our own.

We shall proceed with the topic of revelation, introduced earlier in connection with criteria for determining truth. Who was Jesus? Popular misconceptions abound in the media, but he was neither the conniving pretender described in Hugh Schonfield's immensely popular *The Passover Plot* nor the cowardly collaborator of the infamous film *The Last Temptation of Christ*. We carefully sketch Jesus as revealed to us in the biblical text in order to throw him into bold relief for those getting an increasingly blurred perception.

Having established Jesus' credentials, we turn to his witness to the truthfulness of Scripture. We do not start with the biblical witness as such, which would seem to reason in circular fashion. But we do press on to consider the authenticating importance of miracles as a testimony to revelation.

This will bring us to consider the claims of Christianity in connection with other religious alternatives. The issue seems especially acute as our world shrinks in size, and immigrants of diverse cultural and religious persuasion arrive in North America in increasing numbers. (William Dyrness's *Christian Apologetics in a World Community* serves as a striking case in point of these trends.[1])

WHAT WE ARE HOPING TO FIND

What do we ultimately hope to find? We want to discover if there is a case for Christianity. In the final chapter, we will examine all the evidence and consider the fundamental question: Is Christianity credible?

This reminds me of beginning my doctoral studies at a secular university. While my faith had been cultivated in a Christian college and seminary, I knew many people who had attended secular schools and had fallen prey to demeaning instructors in such an environment. I was especially concerned over the potentially destructive impact of "higher critical" studies on the Bible and in the arena of comparative religions. Eventually, I was greatly relieved to find that the Christian faith stood up to the rigorous test of advanced studies.

WHEN WE HAVE SUCCEEDED
Finally, when shall we know that we have genuinely succeeded? We will know that the apologetic case has been made when we come to obediently trust Christ—when our mind, will, and emotions blend together in wholehearted response to his call to radical discipleship.

The challenge is before us. Let's begin to weigh the evidence and see what kind of case develops.

CHAPTER 1

What Is Truth?

A LL who love the truth recognize that what I say is true," Jesus boldly proclaimed to Pilate in defending his claim to be the king of the Jews (John 18:37). "What is truth?" was the classic response of the Roman governor in the midst of his interrogation of Jesus. However, seemingly without exploring the matter further, Pilate turned on his heels and went to speak with those demanding Jesus' execution. He did not have time to ponder the question of the ages. He was a practical man worried over a social disturbance, with little concern for theoretical matters.

But what is truth? Many have spent their lifetimes in the quest for truth, only to come up empty-handed. Others have dogmatized it on the basis of flimsy evidence. And so the search goes on.

IMMEDIATE CRITERIA

The young man was adamant: "The Bible is the basis for my belief and practice!" "As interpreted by whom?" I inquired. He immediately assumed a defensive stance. It turned out that he interpreted Scripture through the doctrinal grid of religious literature that seriously distorted the results.

How are we to distinguish truth from error? Warren Young

(A Christian Approach to Philosophy) suggests four types of criteria for evaluating truth.[1] He labels the first of these immediate criteria. *Instinct* serves as a case in point. Instinct is thought to be an inborn trait. We refer to religious instinct, by which we mean that people are inherently religious.

If we could establish beyond a reasonable doubt that people are inherently religious, this would be an important discovery. However, it is exceedingly difficult to demonstrate, even though there may be substantial evidence to support the conclusion. Perhaps, more to the point, it is virtually impossible to distinguish instinct from learned behavior, for the two are characteristically expressed together.

Feeling is another example of immediate criteria. Feelings incorporate a wide range of experience. We say that we feel cold when a chilling breeze comes in off the lake. We report that we feel depressed when our plans fail to materialize. We rationalize some action on the basis of a hunch (feeling), rather than having carefully thought through the matter.

Feelings are notorious for being misleading. We may feel that someone has rejected us when that is not the case. One may feel like the hit of the party, when others think him a bore. Feelings are profoundly influenced by such things as our state of health and weather conditions.

Sense experience provides a third illustration of immediate criteria. We assume that what our senses report is, in fact, true. We confidently assert, "I saw it with my own eyes." Anything short of our witnessing the event is, by implication, suspect.

However, a careful distinction needs to be made. It is one thing to say that the senses are the means through which we gather much of our knowledge and quite another to hold them up as the final standard for truth. Recall how a pole appears bent in the water as we observe it, but, when removed, the bend disappears. It only seemed bent because of the refraction of light.

Intuition concludes our brief survey of immediate criteria. It alludes to some means of direct communication that does not require we weigh the matter further. Intuition precludes a deliberate reasoning process.

Recent studies seem to suggest that feminine intuition results from a freer cooperation among the component parts of the brain. This does not necessarily imply a better grasp of truth than the male alternative, but only a different operation. Even if we could build a case for intuition as a truth criterion, we could not exclude complementary means. The axiom "all truth is intuitive" is in fact a truth claim that cannot be established on intuitive grounds alone. It is actually a reasoned conclusion.

This reminds me of the example of an enthusiastic young woman visiting the Mamertine Prison in Rome. "I just know this is the place Paul was imprisoned," she gushed. She needed no evidence other than what she felt, nor did the disbelief of her academic mentor dissuade her. This is the way immediate criteria operate.

As appealing as the case for immediate criteria may at first appear, something more is obviously necessary in the quest for truth. We need not ignore immediate criteria, as if they had no bearing on the quest for truth, but neither should we uncritically trust them as altogether trustworthy. We need to search further in our quest for truth.

SOCIAL CRITERIA

We turn now from immediate to social criteria. What help can we derive from our social experience in the quest for truth?

Custom provides an obvious case in point. The basis on

which society operates is alleged as true. We sometimes refer to this as conventional wisdom, or, in a more popular vein, as tradition. We put our confidence in the accumulated legacy of the past, refined in a social setting.

One problem with this approach is that traditions clash with one another. In addition, traditions change from time to time, suggesting that something was lacking in our previous understanding and perhaps also in our current alternative.

Such realization leads us to an alternative social criterion: *universal consensus*. This latter option seems more appealing in that it draws upon not one culture but humanity as a whole.

This would, in fact, be a more promising alternative if consensus could be more easily demonstrated, but this is seldom, if ever, the case. Moreover, popular views have repeatedly been repudiated, such as the idea that the world is flat. It may appear flat and be assumed flat without actually being flat.

A distressed young student came to my office with a problem concerning her term project. It seemed that she had reached a conclusion different from that commonly accepted. I looked over her research, which appeared thoroughly accurate. By successfully challenging a long-standing consensus, she had effectively demonstrated the limited effectiveness of social criteria as a means of establishing truth.

While social criteria provides some means for comparing our understanding of truth with others, the results are less than assuring. We come to realize that not only individuals but groups can be mistaken. Truth remains an illusive commodity even when the quest takes on a social dimension.

PHILOSOPHIC CRITERIA
Some have pursued the quest for truth with more rigor than others. It seems possible and perhaps even probable that they

4

might have gained greater insight than the average person. With this possibility in mind, let's look at various philosophic options which have been introduced to refine the search for truth.

Correspondence is a prime example of philosophic criteria. Truth is what corresponds to reality. So far so good, but the problem is not so easily solved. It is one thing to assert that truth is what corresponds to reality, but quite another thing to determine the nature of reality. The proposition serves better as a definition than a determination.

We do not have to look far before coming up with an alternative philosophic criterion in *pragmatism*. It defines truth in terms of practicality, whether something brings about satisfactory results in everyday life. We might say that something becomes true in that we discover that it works.

The limitations of this option can be demonstrated in a number of ways. For instance, such an approach fragments the quest for truth. We need to inquire for whom it is true, under what circumstances, and within what framework of thinking. We might be advised in this instance to replace the notion of truth with relevance, which seems more to the point. In addition, this is another case in which the basic assumption falls outside the means of verification.

As a final example of philosophic criteria, we consider *coherence*. Young cites the position of Edgar Sheffield Brightman, with whom I studied briefly, as a case in point.[2] Brightman suggests that our quest for truth should include consistence (within ourselves), inclusiveness (all pertinent factors being considered), organization (arranged in a proper fashion), hypothesis (the formulation of a tentative explanation), and verification (adoption of the explanation as probably true). His impressive system is obviously indebted to the scientific model and draws from it an initial sense of credibility.

5

However, it also inherits the inherent weaknesses of that model. While the scientific method works well in instances where carefully controlled and repeatable experiments can be carried out, it is not, as a rule, considered adequate as a general method of verification. For instance, coherence operates better in natural sciences than social sciences. It offers at best a tentative or partial explanation, which may be revised in terms of a paradigm shift (see Thomas Kuhn, *The Structure of Scientific Revolutions*[3]). Young concludes that the coherence criterion "is measured by observation which takes place through the colored spectacles with which reality is grasped."[4]

I recall a skeptical graduate student sitting across the living room from me. He claimed to have insurmountable problems with believing in the existence of God. Our conversation continued on for more than an hour. One concern after another seemed satisfied, whereupon he lapsed into silence. "Have you other difficulties with believing that God exists?" I finally asked. "No," he replied as if disappointed. It was as if reason had brought him to the threshold of conviction, but no further.

We are deeply indebted to philosophic considerations as an adjunct to the immediate and social criteria. Perhaps they have taken us as far as we can go by our own efforts. Here we are likely to sense as never before our finite limitations. We may even feel some sympathy for Pilate as he turned away from Jesus' invitation to the question for truth. He may well have felt that little more could be said than had already been said better by others.

REVELATION

There is perhaps another alternative remaining open to us. Some faiths, including Christianity, affirm revelation as a truth criterion. The Christian reasons that if humans are made in the image of God, to seek for truth apart from God's guidance is to admit failure from the outset. Without reliance on God's revelation, we cannot hope to fit life into its proper framework.

Even so, we must approach any claim for revelation with care. A matronly woman once offered to share with me her alleged communication with Christ. "What did he have to say?" I skeptically inquired. "He has been making good progress since joining the spirit world," she confidently replied. It seemed obvious to me that her communicant was not to be identified with the biblical Christ.

The notion of revelation casts the interchange between Pilate and Jesus in a strikingly different light. Jesus asserted that it was his mission to bear witness to the truth: "I came to bring truth to the world" (John 18:37). This would, of course, include the idea that what he taught was true.

Jesus' claim involved not only speaking the truth but concerned his messianic calling in particular. It had been a matter of considerable discussion as to what effect the coming of the Messiah would have with regard to the revered Torah—the Jewish wisdom and law. The consensus was that while the Torah would still be in effect, it would be recast in the light of Messiah's advent. The details appeared uncertain. In this connection, Jesus asserted that he was timely truth (truth as realized with the coming of Christ).

Such truth was not in any way meant to subvert the truth of God as had been previously revealed. God does not say one thing on one occasion and retract it on another. Jesus declared: "I do nothing on my own, but I speak what the Father taught me" (John 8:28). He thereby emphasized continuity in divine revelation.

The most astonishing dimension of Jesus' revelatory claims

was in connection with his use of the theophany formula "I am" (John 8:58; cf. Exodus 3:14). These were the words uttered to Moses from the burning bush and which Jesus appropriated for himself. His was a claim to incarnate truth: the truth of God embodied in human flesh.

We will delve more into these remarkable claims in a later chapter; suffice, for now, to say it is unique in the annals of history. In fact, C. S. Lewis once remarked that it was what appealed most to him about Christianity. He felt that this claim was not something that humans would have imagined on their own, as it differed so sharply from the predictable pattern of religious myth.

It seems evident that humanity with its finite capacity would be limited in the quest for truth. Scripture incorporates this religious/moral culpability in portraying humanity separated from God by an expanse as great as the heavens are above the earth (Isaiah 55:8-9). We would despair unless God should take the initiative to reveal the nature of truth to us.

Our dilemma may be illustrated by an enthusiastic college dropout I once encountered. He testified to discovering in his mystical pilgrimage what he had failed to uncover in his formal education. "It is fantastic!" he exclaimed. It was indeed "fantastic," but not in the way he intended. His beliefs defied any serious effort at verification. They were strange and even absurd.

We ought not to take leave of our sanity in the search for truth. We should use whatever means God has put at our disposal. But do not mistake faith for credulity.

Pilate had what seemed to him more pressing things with which to be concerned. He had satisfied himself that Jesus was no dangerous revolutionary. Now, he had either to convince the crowd or submit to their demands. If there was one thing imperial Rome would not tolerate, it was disturbance of the

Pax Romana (the Peace of Rome). If necessary, this troublesome rabbi would be sacrificed to retain public order.

One is struck by the contrast between Jesus' and Pilate's attitudes toward the quest for truth. The former took it seriously; the latter was more interested in finding an expedient course of action. I suppose that a study of apologetics, Christian or otherwise, would appeal to those who take the quest for truth seriously. They would be interested, not only in the claims made by rival faiths, but the reasons advanced for believing them to be true. They would be adverse to narrow viewpoints and hope to achieve some comprehensive understanding of the world in which they live.

If God gave us a mind, no doubt he intended us to use it. We ought not to claim more for our investigative powers than our finite condition warrants, but even so, these provide us with some means to evaluate rival claims to revealed truth. We are left to consider with Pilate Jesus' claim to bear witness to the truth. We certainly cannot afford to take it lightly and still profess to take up the quest for truth in earnest.

We have made a beginning. Our quest has closed some doors and opened others. We need to pursue the opportunities made available. This leads us in the following chapter to consider the role of religious experience. In apologetics, it is a subject so critical that some virtually exclude all other considerations. They err in doing so. We will use this important topic as a stepping-stone to other related matters in our case.

DISCUSSION QUESTIONS

1. Why may some have believed what Jesus had to say concerning truth and others have rejected it? How differently may he have appeared to his Jewish disciples, those Jews who agitated for his execution, and Gentiles such as Pilate?

2. Some rely heavily on immediate criteria for validating what they believe. What illustrations come to mind? What is deficient in an apologetic based essentially on immediate criteria?

3. Can you identify any faiths that put especially strong emphasis on the social criteria in their apologetic? What are the strengths and weaknesses of an apologetic developed in such a fashion?

4. "From the time the world was created, people have seen the earth and sky and all that God made. They can clearly see his invisible qualities—his eternal power and divine nature. So they have no excuse whatsoever for not knowing God" (Romans 1:20). What are the implications of this verse for the quest for truth?

5. In some sense Jesus *was* and *is* the Christian apologetic. What does this conclusion imply for your study of Christian apologetics?

CHAPTER 2

Experiencing God

I T is one thing to believe that God exists; it is quite another to claim you have encountered him. Religious experience crosses age, sex, educational level, social status, and cultural barriers. It occurs with such frequency and with such tenacity as to be admitted as theistic evidence (belief in a personal deity).

This does not imply that we necessarily take such religious testimonies at face value. Some profess not to have religious experience, and others seek to explain it on naturalistic grounds. We can still maintain a healthy skepticism without minimizing the potential apologetic value of religious reports.

RELIGIOUS EXPERIENCE

To help us better understand the area of religious experience we need to stand on the shoulders of those who have gone before us. First, we will consider William James, whose *The Varieties of Religious Experience* (1902)[1] has long been acknowledged as a standard work on religious experience. Subsequent authors have felt free to take issue with, but not to neglect, this classic resource. We will look closely at his classifications, use of source material, and treatment of conversion.

James differentiated between mild and intense religious experience. Mild experience may be characterized as a confident sense of God's presence. Preachers sometimes encourage their parishioners to "practice the presence of God." They mean that we should live in confident trust of God's providential care throughout the changing fortunes of life.

I fondly recall a man who exemplified such an attitude. His face always seemed bathed in contentment. He never seemed distressed, anxious, or impatient. It seemed likely that he was experiencing God's presence as if it were an ongoing benediction.

On the other hand, an intense variety of religious experience reflects a transport into the presence of God. We may pass from a sense of abject alienation, through confession and cleansing, to reconciliation and communion with the Almighty. We climb a ladder from the "dark night of the soul" to the brilliance of God's glory. These are the more memorable religious experiences to which people refer back and draw consolation.

Still vivid in my memory is an occasion at the end of one school year. I felt thoroughly exhausted and somewhat dejected. Traveling with our five small children for a family holiday, we pulled into a campground. Pulling myself into a sleeping bag not meant to accommodate my six-foot-three-inch frame, I had to contend with ravenous and persistent mosquitoes for the remainder of the night.

When at last morning came, I arose for a solitary walk by the lakeshore. It seemed that real and imagined problems weighed down my every footstep. Then, when the sun broke into full view, I felt a tremendous release. It was as if to appreciate that God was still sovereign and all was well with those who love him and trust their ways to him.

We sometimes refer to such occasions as "mountaintop

experiences." Although the struggle up the slope may have been difficult, the result proves well worth the effort.

James assumed, for all practical purposes, that religious experience was cut from the same cloth, regardless of the particular confession. He chose his illustrations of mild and extreme religious experience from a broad range of religious faiths, which, at least initially, might suggest that they tell us more about the nature of humans than God.

He singled out religious conversion for special treatment. James observed that while some appear to require a second birth in order to integrate their otherwise fragmented psyche, others seemed healthy and well-adjusted from the outset—not requiring so radical a transformation. Nineteenth-century clergyman Horace Bushnell stated as the Christian ideal to raise children so that they could never remember a time when they were not Christians, anticipating James's once-born thesis.[2]

Sven Norberg countered James with a relatively unknown work *(Varieties of Christian Experience)* meant to point out the distinctive nature of Christian experience.[3] He argued that Christ is the objective sine qua non (indispensable condition) of the Christian experience. While resembling other religious experience from a human perspective, it is unique from a theological perspective.

This brings to mind an exceptional instance which, for that very reason, perhaps best illustrates Norberg's thesis. A sociology class at a local university decided to attend an evangelistic service as a group project. Some would sit near the front of the auditorium and cooperate by singing lustily, following the Scripture reading, and listening attentively. Others would sit in obscure locations and disassociate themselves from the proceedings. Afterward, they would compare their experiences in the light of anticipated results.

Much to virtually everyone's surprise, one of the students made a decision for Christ. Only one person, himself a believer, seemed to grasp what had transpired. He had also experienced the transforming power of the gospel.

It is obvious that people have religious experiences. The question is whether we are correct in identifying them with God, or can they be explained in some other fashion? Skeptics suggest that the religious experience is generated either psychologically or sociologically, rather than religiously.

Sigmund Freud argued that religion is the projection of wish thinking. The Viennese psychologist reasoned that life proves hard for humankind to endure. There is always some degree of privation; others afflict us from time to time; our aspirations fall far short of realization. As a result, we attempt to "humanize" life, to discover meaning and purpose. In the end, we invent God. Freud elaborated:

> If the elements have passions that rage as they do in our own soul, if death itself is not something spontaneous but the violent act of an evil will, if everywhere in nature there are Beings around us of a kind that we know in our own society, then we can breathe freely, we can feel at home in the uncanny and can deal by psychical means with our senseless anxiety.[4]

In our response to Freud, the fact that we wish something to be true may as readily imply that it is true as that it is not. Moreover, the rigor and sacrifice associated with the Christian life is not what we would assume people to have wished for. Finally, the conclusion that God does not exist could as plausibly result from Freud's wishes that wishing this were so.

As if to illustrate my point, an acquaintance once said, "I would prefer that God does not exist. It would allow me to live life as I please." Few are so candid, but I suspect that the attitude is far more pervasive than we might surmise. Wish-fulfillment may be a sword that cuts both ways, to establish the existence or the demise of God.

Sociologist Emile Durkheim's classic work, *The Elementary Forms of Religious Life* (1956), suggests that religion is the mythological manner in which a people promotes social order. He reasoned that religion is not an accidental element of society but is, rather, its substance. Without religion in some form, society could not exist.[5]

Durkheim emphasizes the importance of the "collective representations" of society. These relate to the collection of meanings, ideas, and values which hold society together. They are expressed as divine sanctions to further corporate human ends.

It would seem that Durkheim confuses function with fact. While beliefs may serve social ends, it does not follow that they were created solely for that purpose. Certainly, those who believe in God do not understand their faith in that manner.

The biblical prophets distinguished between the living God and the pagan gods created for social advantage. They appealed to the Hebrew people to transcend personal interests, often at considerable corporate risk, to serve a sovereign God. Such experiences would seem difficult to reconcile with Durkheim's thesis of social accommodation.

The basic contention of the skeptic, whether of psychological or sociological bent, is that religious experience can be explained as human projection. It seems to the theist more than a little presumptuous to think that humans can be credited with so profound and unrelenting an experience. It likewise appears reductionistic to explain theology as anthropology.

ALL AND NOTHING BUT THE TRUTH

Not all witnesses are equally credible. Philosopher C. Stephen Evans sets forth two basic criteria for credibility: (1) The observer must be qualified, and (2) the conditions must be favorable. Evans breaks down the former into three categories: (1) the individual must be attentive and seeking, (2) certain recognition skills may be required, and (3) the quality of life and purpose is of critical importance.[6]

First, the individual must be attentive and seeking. Scripture promised the Hebrews: "If you search for him with all your heart and soul, you will find him" (Deuteronomy 4:29). No halfhearted effort would do. Jesus likened the kingdom of heaven to a merchant who, when he found a pearl of great value, sold everything he had so that he might purchase it (Matthew 13:45-46). Such must be the importance we assign to the search for God, to gladly count the loss of all little enough to succeed.

The decision is not something we can afford to postpone. Other matters may be put off without seriously affecting life. Not so with the religious quest. It is a concern of utmost importance.

Second, certain recognition skills may be required. I suspect that this is what C. S. Lewis had in mind when he tied the experience of the *numinous* (sensing God's presence) to fear of ghosts, and, in turn, to fear of tigers.[7] In reverse order, we may sharpen our recognition skills by reflecting on the fear we experience concerning wild animals, introduce a supernatural aspect by substituting ghosts, and finish off with a sovereign Spirit, who controls our life and destiny.

The apologist hoped in this way to prime people suspect of the supernatural to open themselves to God's initiatives. He wanted them to let down the naturalistic barriers and open up their windows toward heaven.

Third, the quality of life and purpose is also of critical importance. The apostle Paul wrote: "I want men to pray with holy hands lifted up to God, free from anger and controversy" (1 Timothy 2:8). Jesus taught that if one is offering a gift at the altar and remembers that his brother has something against him, he should go first and be reconciled to his brother (Matthew 5:23-24). Only then, after setting his life in order and being able to worship in good conscience, should he complete his offering to God.

Some press ahead without proper preparation. "I would be genuinely interested in knowing whether God exists," the young intellectual observed. He was only interested in satisfying his curiosity but not in acknowledging God's claim on his life. He was, for that reason, a poor candidate for an encounter with the Almighty.

Evans incisively concludes: "If God's reality were too obvious, it would be difficult for even selfish men and women to avoid obeying his laws, for it would be the height of foolishness to challenge an omnipotent, omniscient being."[8] It seems reasonable that God would remain hidden to those who resist his will and despise his grace.

As noted above, not only must the observer be qualified, but the conditions must be favorable. Evans freely admits: "It is, if anything, even more difficult to say when the objective conditions for experiencing God have been satisfied."[9] God is not passive in the situation, but takes the initiative. He selects the time, occasion, and means at his disposal. We may do better in retrospect. We see, or think we see, how God has been providentially working in our life, while, at the time, we were perhaps confused or even surprised by some turn of events.

We accept most of what we hold as true based on the witness of others. We normally assume their experiences to be credible unless there are substantial reasons for not doing so. This is especially so when the witnesses appear trustworthy and the circumstances under which they operate seem optimum. Given this generally accepted approach, a strong case can be built for theism on the basis of personal witness.

FOCUS IN RESULTS

If there is a God, and if he is of the righteous character generally assumed, we would expect an encounter with him to normally achieve wholesome results. David Larson, in an interview several years ago, reported that clinical counselors, as a rule, continue to treat religious experience negatively even though the evidence shows that it tends to yield positive results.

Larson, who served on the staff of the National Institute of Mental Health and now acts as a consultant for the National Institute for Healthcare Research, reports that nineteen of twenty studies demonstrate that religious experience acts as a preventive against alcoholism; sixteen of sixteen studies showed that it reduced the frequency of suicide; studies also indicated lower incidences of mental health problems and even lower blood pressure (taking into consideration other variables).

Religious experience likewise proved to be an incentive to health-related behavior such as exercise, resting, prayer, and meditation. It was also found to promote quicker recovery from a range of illnesses, from emotional disorders to hip fractures among the elderly.

Religiously oriented people, likewise, express a greater satisfaction with life. They generally hold a more positive attitude toward their personal life and association with others. Larson concludes that healthy religious people can be characterized as having a genuine commitment to God, somewhat flexible and open to change, and willing to admit they need assistance from others.

Religious experience has also been shown to have constructive social results. The most important factor in enabling African-American males to escape the urban ghetto was not excelling in athletics, but active participation in church life. This was also the major determinant in whether they returned to help others.

Larson, nevertheless, saw reason for concern. Some studies seem to indicate that marginal believers actually are less emotionally healthy than their secular counterparts. A pronounced contradiction between expressed beliefs and actual practice puts a heavy stress on emotional health. Research has also shown that a broken home constitutes a serious health hazard.

Religious experience can, according to Larson, be fine-tuned to gain maximum results. He recommends that we work at living out what we claim to believe, give ourselves time to think and pray about matters, attend church regularly, practice spiritual disciplines, and live courageously—working out our personal calling with enthusiasm.

Evans moves to bring the topic to conclusion: "The skeptic may here retort that God would presumably want everyone to know about himself and should therefore be expected to reveal himself to all. The believer's response to this is that God has revealed himself to all; a general revelation of God is available in nature and conscience."[10] God can hardly be blamed if we choose to explain our religious experience on naturalistic grounds or fail to use such light as we have in search of a personal encounter.

As a matter of fact, religious believers assume that others can duplicate their experiences. They share their testimonies confidently, with anticipation that, if the seeker is earnest, God will reward his or her effort. This has been their own experience, and they have witnessed similar results in the lives of others.

Now that we have introduced the role of religious experience in Christian belief, we need to look more closely at how others have sought to defend the faith throughout church history. The next two chapters will provide a brief, but necessary, history of apologetics.

DISCUSSION QUESTIONS

1. Most of what we accept as true is based on the witness of others. Why do people, therefore, find it so difficult to accept religious testimonies?
2. In what ways might Christian experience differ and yet be similar to the experience reported by those of other faiths? Reflect on William James's observations in this context.
3. Reread Paul's experience as recorded in Acts 9. What implications can be drawn for apologetic purposes?
4. What sort of evidence do we have that religious experience translates into a healthy lifestyle? What is the apologetic value of such evidence?
5. Compare your religious experience with others. What do you make of the similarities and differences?

CHAPTER 3

Apologetics through the Ages

NEARLY two thousand years have passed since Jesus stood before Pilate. The church has grown from what at first appeared as an insignificant Jewish sect to a faith unrivaled in universal appeal, number of adherents, and impact on society at large. Apologetic precedents have been set, refined, and extended in the process.

JESUS AS AN APOLOGIST

Christian apologetics began with Jesus. Others have attempted to steer by the course he set. Judaism was at Jesus' time a richly varied mosaic. There were various parties; these included the Pharisees, Sadducees, Essenes, and Zealots. There were also Gentiles living in Palestine, many of whom had been relocated there long ago by the Assyrians and Babylonians.

This proliferation of Jewish groups primarily resulted from the introduction of Hellenism (Greek thought) into the culture. The Hellenic spirit had captured the imagination of the Roman Empire, and Israel was not entirely immune. Some Jews urged compliance, and others promoted resistance—with a range of positions resulting.

Jesus' apologetic was expressed in the context of Jewish

sectarianism. It seems more often than not set over against the Pharisees, which appear as the sect most in contact with the followers of Jesus. His Sermon on the Mount (Matthew 5–7) has even been described as an "anti-Pharisaic manifesto." In any case, he carried on a sustained and sometimes heated debate with the Pharisees.

Jesus had relatively little contact with the Sadducees. They were the party of the privileged, and Jesus was an advocate for the common person. The Jewish historian Josephus reports that they were unable to convince anyone but the rich of their cause. Jesus collided with their invested interest when he cleansed the temple, precipitating his crucifixion.

There were efforts to enlist Jesus in the struggle against Rome. Galilee was at the time the center of the Zealots, a radical fringe group capable of soliciting popular support. The Zealots refused to give allegiance to Caesar or to pay the required taxes. Jesus declared that his kingdom was not of this world, thereby rejecting their political overtures.

While noticeable by their absence from the biblical record, the separatistic character of the Essenes sharply contrasted with the teachings of Jesus. They were ascetic, legalistic, ritualistic, and exclusivistic: positions which Jesus relentlessly assailed by word and practice.

Jesus expressed remarkable compassion toward the common people. He portrayed God as a loving father, who longs for the return of his prodigal son. The Pharisees resembled the elder brother, who does not share his father's forgiving nature. Such was the sectarian context in which Jesus expressed his apologetic.

Jesus' apologetic focused on his messianic calling. He was named before birth, in keeping with messianic expectation, and his messianic identity was validated by the Resurrection. His intervening life was punctured with messianic allusions, such as the feeding of the thousands, healing of the infirm, and control over the natural elements.

Jesus cautioned his disciples not to speak publicly of his messianic identity lest his ministry be misunderstood and so as to allow time for clarification. The Jews distinguished between the present age and the age to come (the messianic age). Jesus announced that he had inaugurated the messianic era, which must run its course. That is to say, the midpoint had passed. Jesus was and is the messianic agent of the new era, and to this end he put his apologetic energies. Perhaps a diagram would help:

Jewish view of history:
the present age/the age to come
(as yet future)

Christian modification:
the present age/the age to come
(now inaugurated)

As we noted in chapter 2, of special concern was the relation of the Torah (Old Testament teaching, law) to the new situation. It was common knowledge that while the Torah would not be set aside during the messianic age, it would reflect the change in circumstances. Jesus emphasized the basic principles of Torah: wholehearted love of God and love of neighbor as self, rather than meticulous obsession with ritual trivia. He severely rebuked his opposition when they rejected Scripture in order to placate tradition.

Jesus set out to reconcile the various strains of messianic prophecy. The Qumran community (a monastic group that produced the Dead Sea Scrolls) had attempted to do so by introducing two messiahs: one who would die and be revived by the other. Jesus related these prophecies to himself, asserting that he would die, be raised from the dead, ascend into heaven, and return to complete his messianic calling. There was an unrelenting messianic thrust to his apologetic.

New Testament Apologetics

The New Testament writers picked up where Jesus left off. The Gospels resemble an overlay: the recollections of the life of Christ as they related to apostolic times. The authors felt obligated to address two remarkable developments: (1) the Jewish rejection of Jesus as the Messiah, and (2) the rapid expansion of Christianity in Gentile circles. They had to account for apparent failure where success might have been anticipated and success where more modest results might have sufficed.

While the Gospels are, without exception, concerned with establishing Jesus' claim as Messiah, John was the most explicit. "But these are written so that you may believe that Jesus is the Messiah, the Son of God, and that by believing in him you will have life" (John 20:31). John begins with Jesus turning water to wine at the marriage feast in Cana and concludes with the Resurrection. Those who demanded an authenticating sign of Jesus (Matthew 12:38) had either been unaware of or had dismissed the cumulative evidence already available. Jesus replied that no other sign would be given but that of the prophet Jonah: As he had been three days and nights in the stomach of the great fish, so would the Son of Man be in the heart of the earth (Matthew 12:39-40).

Sectarian Judaism was no longer in the foreground by this time. John refers to "the Jews" as a corporate ethnic people characterized by rejection of Jesus as the Messiah, even though he himself was a believing Jew. Judas, who left the upper room and went out into the night, graphically represented for John the Jewish plight.

"But despite all the miraculous signs he had done, most of the people did not believe in him" (John 12:37). John observes that this was to fulfill the prophecy of Isaiah concerning their eyes being blinded and hearts hardened. He adds that many, nevertheless, did believe, including leaders among the people who failed to speak out for fear of reprisal.

John weaves the response theme together with rejection. Whosoever will may come; whoever comes to Jesus will not be cast aside; threats will not deter those of dauntless faith. John continues to hold out hope for those who will consider the evidence impartially.

Paul was another noteworthy apologist. He made a practice of going to the Jew first and turning to the Gentile only when his prior efforts proved fruitless. His address at Pisidian Antioch (Acts 13:14-41) was representative of his approach to the Jew, and that at Athens (Acts 17:22-31), to the Gentile. The former took advantage of a common Jewish historical legacy, and the latter built upon general revelation.

Paul stated as his modus operandi: "I am not bound to obey people just because they pay me, yet I have become a servant of everyone so that I can bring them to Christ" (1 Corinthians 9:19). To the Jews, he became as a Jew; to the Gentiles, he acted as a Gentile. "I do all this to spread the Good News, and in doing so I enjoy its blessings" (1 Corinthians 9:23).

The apostle added proclamation to accommodation:

> So where does this leave the philosophers, the scholars, and the world's brilliant debaters? God has made them all look foolish and has shown their wisdom to be useless nonsense. . . . God's way seems foolish to the Jews because they want a sign from heaven to prove it

is true. And it is foolish to the Greeks because they believe only what agrees with their own wisdom. So when we preach that Christ was crucified, the Jews are offended, and the Gentiles say it's all nonsense. But to those called by God to salvation, both Jews and Gentiles, Christ is the mighty power of God and the wonderful wisdom of God. (1 Corinthians 1:20, 22-24)

Paul introduced teaching and admonition along with proclamation. "So everywhere we go, we tell everyone about Christ. We warn them and teach them with all the wisdom God has given us, for we want to present them to God, perfect in their relationship to Christ" (Colossians 1:28).

Along with the rest, Paul insisted on verification. He drew upon the religious and moral experience of his Athenian audience before concluding: "For [God] has set a day for judging the world with justice by the man he has appointed, and he proved to everyone who this is by raising him from the dead" (Acts 17:31). The Resurrection was the capstone to the apostle's case for Christianity.

The book of Hebrews provides a striking example of New Testament apologetics. Its author elaborates the superiority of the new covenant of Christ over the old covenant of the law. Well versed in philosophical matters, he appears to employ the Platonic distinction between what is seen as temporal as over against what is unseen and eternal. In the process, he refutes the opposition, forges a Christian alternative, and provides an apologetic bridge between the two.

The Christian movement soon drew the attention of Roman magistrates. Paul, having defended himself before Felix and Festus, appealed his case to Caesar. The New Testament writers represent the officials, as a rule, as being contentious, on one occasion seeking personal gain, and predictably concerned to preserve the *Pax Romana*.

As for Christians, they are commended as being earnest, law-abiding, and devout. They strive to live what they preach and preach what they have come to believe on compelling evidence.

EARLY CHURCH APOLOGETICS

Subsequent apologetics took its cue from the New Testament. Justin Martyr (100–165) provides a classic case in point. Justin was born in the region of Samaria, and his writings reveal familiarity with a wide range of pagan philosophy. He reports to have studied Stoicism, Aristotelianism, Pythagoreanism, and Platonism before embracing Christianity. His conversion came about as a result of talking with an elderly believer. Justin recalls that although he never saw the man again, "My spirit was immediately set on fire, and affection for the prophets, and for those who are friends of Christ, took hold of me; while pondering on his words, I discovered that his was the only sure and useful philosophy."[1] He subsequently set up his own private school in Rome.

Justin wrote two apologies, along with his dialogue with Trypho the Jew. He stated as his purpose: "It is for us to offer to all the opportunity of inspecting our life and teachings, lest we ourselves should bear the blame for what those who do not really know about us do in this ignorance."[2]

The apologist introduced several lines of reasoning, of which we will mention four: the logos doctrine, Christian life, civil obedience, and symbolism. He held that "the true light, who gives light to everyone" (John 1:9) implies a general revelation of Christ through imparted reason. Thus, he concluded if one were genuinely to live according to reason, he or she would be a Christian. This conviction allowed Justin to draw upon such insights as he found in pagan writers to support his claims.

Justin also contrasted the noble life of Christians to their pagan contemporaries as evidence for the credibility of the faith. He argued that Socrates set forth an ideal which only Christians approximate in reality. Justin also refuted pagan charges, such as that the Christians were atheists. They were atheistic only in that they refuted false gods in order to worship the living God.

The matter of civil obedience was also crucial to Justin's apologetic. He appealed to the emperor not to judge Christians according to hearsay, but by proper investigation. Although citizens of a spiritual kingdom, Christians were obedient to established authority. If, contrary to the apologist's appeal, Christians were called upon to suffer for their faith, Justin was of the opinion that they could be killed but not harmed.

Justin dwelt at length on God's preparation of culture for the reception of the gospel, as evidenced in symbols of redemption. He seemed to find the cross at every turn: the mast of a boat put to sea, man as he stands erect with arms extended, and even the bridge of one's nose.

Justin's comments to Trypho are likewise of apologetic interest. He reasoned that those who devoutly obeyed Mosaic revelation would be redeemed: "Since they who did those things which are universally, naturally and eternally good are pleasing to God, they shall be saved."[3] Yet, redemption would be accomplished only in Christ, for neither they nor we are genuinely able to fulfill the conditions of the Torah.

As for those who wish to keep Jewish ritual practices as a means of identifying with their ethnic tradition, Justin thought this appropriate. Providing, of course, that they do not do so as a means of obtaining salvation. Justin held that those who professed to believe and then turned back into Judaism would be lost.

Tertullian (160–220) carried on Justin's concern for the imperial treatment of Christians. He was born in Carthage. His father was a proconsular centurion. He describes his early life as given over to the brutalities of the arena and vulgarities of the theater. However, these did not deter him from diligent study of literature, law, and philosophy. While the circumstances of his conversion are unknown, he was thought to have been influenced by the faithful witness of the Christian martyrs.

The learned Tertullian took as his apologetic task to refute charges of immorality, infanticide, gluttony, and atheism. He likewise pointed out the charitable character of Christians toward one another: "We hold all in common except our wives."[4]

Tertullian demonstrated little sympathy for pagan philosophy. "What indeed has Athens to do with Jerusalem?" he contemptuously inquired. "With our faith, we require no further research."[5]

We conclude our brief excursion into the apologetics of the early church with the remarkable Augustine (354–430). He was also born in North Africa, of a pagan father and Christian mother. Augustine was thoroughly exposed to the pagan thought of his time and driven by sensual desires. The powerful sermons of Bishop Ambrose, coupled with the persistent prayers of his mother, Monica, eventually bore fruit in Augustine's conversion. His subsequent impact on the course of Christianity is difficult to overestimate.

As the revered bishop of Hippo, Augustine took on three threats to the church: Manichaeism, Donatism, and Pelagianism. Manichaeism was an eclectic faith, which proved vulnerable to the apologist's incisive logic. He developed in the process the notion of evil as good having gone wrong.

Donatism was an overly rigorous reaction toward those who had defected from the faith during persecution. Augustine appealed for a conciliatory attitude, which recognized the grace of God and the possibility of restoration to favor and service.

The Pelagians argued that the biblical admonition to be perfect (Matthew 5:48) implied that humans had the capability to be so. Augustine responded that grace should not be thought of as a substitute for voluntary compliance, but as its means. In this, as in the above instances, he aptly employed biblical and extrabiblical resources, along with an incisive logic to refute error and promote Christian truth.

Augustine's *City of God* provides a classic instance of Christian apologetics. Herein, he defended Christians from the charge that they were to blame for the trouble befalling Rome. He suggested that the empire must bear its own blame, this not being the first time they had reaped just recompense.

On the other hand, God honored the presence of Christians among them as seen in the unusual clemency shown by the barbarians, the ministry of Christians to the afflicted, the necessity of suffering during war, the lesson of gratitude for temporal good and humility for temporal evil, the need for international justice, and the overriding providence of God. With this masterful stroke, Augustine brought down the curtain on apologetics in the early era and assured an abiding legacy for those who would follow.

DISCUSSION QUESTIONS

1. How does the perception of Jesus as an apologist compare to popular perceptions of him? What lessons can be

learned from his apologetic approach to those he encountered?

2. What is the importance of recognizing the context in which apologetics takes place? How was the context for Jesus' apologetic both similar and dissimilar from that of the New Testament writers?

3. An author imagines two people standing at the foot of the cross, looking up at Jesus. One says to the other: "I have seen more likely messiahs." What is at issue, from an apologetic point of view?

4. What problems were encountered as the Christian faith spread rapidly among Gentiles? How did the early apologists attempt to manage the situation?

5. How might history have turned out differently without the early apologists? It has been said: "If we neglect apologetics, we are only one generation away from extinction." Do you agree? Why or why not?

CHAPTER 4

Apologetics to the Present

IT has been said that there are no new heresies. While this may be true, apologists in each era of church history face new challenges, according to the prevailing cultural ethos. In this chapter we will continue to survey the history of apologetics, observing some familiar concerns, as well as new controversies.

The Christian movement first asserted itself at a time when controversy raged concerning the incursion of Hellenistic culture into Hebrew society. It appeared at first as a relatively insignificant and, perhaps, passing phenomena. Such proved not to be the case.

With the dawn of the Middle Ages (476–1453), Christianity had become the religious catalyst of Western civilization. Where once Christian apologists were called upon to defend a misunderstood and misrepresented faith, they now lent credibility to a generally accepted conviction. Their main objective was not to convince the indifferent and sometimes hostile, but to shore up the confidence and piety of those already sympathetic.

CHRISTENDOM

The apologists assumed no small enterprise in firming up a Christian worldview. Peter Berger and Thomas Luckmann have suggested that verification proceeds along four levels: vernacular, rudimentary and explicit theory, and symbolic universe.[1] Everyday language becomes a means of affirming faith. For instance, when someone sneezes, we say, "God bless you." Few stop to realize the apologetic role such manner of speech plays, but its importance ought not be underestimated.

A Jewish rabbi attempted to explain to me the difference he experienced between living in the United States and Israel: "I felt in the U.S. as if everything in the culture was stacked against me, but in Israel the culture is supportive." I could easily identify, for the matter was reversed for me: the American culture is much more user friendly for me as a Christian.

Theories of any degree of sophistication provide the categories whereby we live. The medieval theorists drew a sharp distinction between clergy and laity, setting up detailed guidelines for their respective responsibilities. Family and civic codes were rigorously developed and promoted. When everyone was in his or her rightful place, then all was thought well in the world.

Symbolic universes provide a comprehensive and integrated view of life. Berger and Luckmann explain, "The symbolic universe is conceived of as the matrix of all socially objectivated and subjectively real meanings; the entire historic society and the entire biography of the individual are seen as events taking place within the universe."[2] Symbolic universes (worldviews) also provide credible explanations for concerns not readily verified by natural means, such as immortality.

Christendom, the social-political expression of the Christian faith, was energetically promoted at every level. The church edifice was the most striking feature of village architecture. Community life centered around church activity. Church bells signaled the time for worship, birth of a child, and death of a loved one.

Church and state were seen as agents of God's will. Each contributed, supported one another, and served a divine purpose. Deviation from the religious norm was viewed as a threat to the sacred order of things and could elicit severe reprisal.

The catalyst for the apologetics of the Middle Ages was belief in the existence of God. Once established beyond a reasonable doubt, everything seemed to fall neatly into place. Christendom would be assured its survival, and, with it, God's bountiful blessing.

One name stands out among the other medieval apologists: the remarkably gifted Thomas Aquinas (1225–1274). Aquinas was born of royalty, his father being the count of Aquino. He was educated at the monastery of Monte Cassino, under the supervision of his uncle, the abbot. Aquinas was a large man with a docile disposition, earning him the unflattering designation "the dumb ox." This distracted in no way from his mental acumen, which was recognized early on by his academic mentors.

Aquinas dedicated his energies to study, teaching, and writing. He was able to draw upon Scripture, the church fathers, and classical tradition to compose his monumental *Summa Theologica* and his lesser known apologetic work, *Summa Contra Gentiles*.

Aquinas's arguments for God's existence are commonly referred to as the "Five Ways":

(1) from human perception of motion to Prime Mover,
(2) from the existence of causation to the First Cause,
(3) from the contingent character of life to the Necessary Being,
(4) from the degrees of value to the Absolute Value,
(5) and from purposefulness to the Divine Designer.

They, nonetheless, follow a common pattern: from sensory data, by way of a cause-effect relationship, to establishing the existence of God:

Sensory data
▼
Cause-effect relationship
▼
Existence of God

Whereas Aquinas labored at great length, we will offer but one common illustration of this type of approach. J. Edwin Orr tells of an experience as he strolled along the beach. He came across a series of holes resembling in outline the various continents. He could have concluded that these were caused by some enterprising crab, but rather thought they were the product of a more intelligent form of life. Soon thereafter, he came across a little girl, spade and bucket in hand, who had been adapting her knowledge of geography to recreational purposes. Orr concluded that the intricate design we observe in the universe would similarly imply a Divine Architect!

Anselm of Canterbury (1033–1109) took a contrasting approach to establishing God's existence. Little is known of his early life. When his mother died, and being unable to get along with his father, Anselm left home at the age of twenty-three. Eventually, he decided to enter the monastery at Bec and advanced quickly in the order. His thirty-year stay at the monastery provided a fertile period for writing.

Anselm was offered, but adamantly refused to accept, the position of archbishop of Canterbury. He wished to continue his scholarly pursuits and felt himself unfit for the secular responsibilities the position would entail. It was said that the English bishops had to pry open his fingers to force the official staff into his hands and literally drag him to the church for induction into the office.

There followed an ongoing struggle between Anselm and the English rulers: the former advocating the freedom of the church to fulfill its calling, and the latter attempting to control the church. It is remarkable that the archbishop could continue his scholarly pursuits under such stressful conditions. He vigorously argued that God is "a being than which nothing greater can be conceived." When challenged that a most-perfect island could exist only in the imagination, he replied that unless the island actually existed, it would not be greater than an actual one. Otherwise stated, Anselm meant that perfection implies existence.

It was not his intent to discover faith itself, but to explore why he believed. Others could and would draw on his insights to foster faith. We might think of this as a by-product of the original purpose. It served as an icing, so to speak, on the apologetic cake.

The "assured results" of medieval apologetics were coming under increased attack well before the dawn of the present era. William of Occam (1285–1349) was a case in point. William argued that we are limited to perceptions of external reality, not knowledge of external reality per se. He went on to affirm that God may be known only by faith.

Medieval apologetics was actually under assault on two fronts: (1) that it attempted to prove too much, thereby usurping the role of faith, and, (2) that what it demonstrated fell pathetically short of the God revealed in Scripture. The theistic arguments were not, strictly speaking, "proofs" at all, but probability arguments based either on sense perception or introspection.

As a matter of record, the medieval apologists never meant to exclude revelation or faith in their emphasis on reason.

Special revelation was important for Aquinas in three ways: (1) concerning God's creation of the world, (2) his plan of redemption, and (3) the doctrine of the Trinity. General revelation was not thought sufficient for any of these.

Aquinas admittedly accented the intellectual aspect of faith. To believe was to think with assent. Faith is inferior to natural reason with reference to evidence; it is superior with regard to the intrinsic value of its object.

"That certain divine truths wholly surpass the capability of human reason, is mostly clearly evident."[3] Nothing, Aquinas insists, is more certain than the Word of God. Reasoning faith in response to divine revelation provides an assured apologetic legacy.

THE MODERN ERA

Christendom was not so deeply rooted or pervasive as is sometimes portrayed. Paganism accommodated as necessary, biding its time and waiting for an occasion to reassert itself. The church also squandered much of its opportunity. It proved much more vulnerable to prosperity than to persecution.

The fourteenth-century Renaissance (revival of classical learning), coupled with the sixteenth-century scientific movement, may be said to have ushered in the modern era. This was the age of the so-called Enlightenment. Humans took center stage, reason was enthroned, and people were encouraged to achieve their full potential. God was given increasingly less serious consideration, and religious constraints were enthusiastically cast aside.

The Reformation resembled more of a family squabble, compared to the challenge of the modern age to traditional Christianity. J. W. S. Reid observes, "The theology of the

Reformation allots a minor role to apologetic activity. In doing so it follows the path already taken by the later medieval theologians."[4] Its renewed emphasis on Scripture also tended to minimize the role of autonomous reason.

Partisan apologetics came to dominate during the Reformation and Counter-Reformation. John Calvin (1509–1564) argued in *The Necessity of Reforming the Church* and *Reply to Sadolet* that he felt compelled to expound the saving truth of the gospel as represented in Scripture, over against the superstitions and errors of an unreformed and unrepentant church. The Roman Catholics countered with an appeal to the apostolic and universal character of the Christian faith. The religious wars that followed attempted to settle by sword what could not be achieved by pen.

Evangelists of the new age were quick to call attention to the suffering caused by religion serving partisan interests. Some went so far as to deride religion as such.

Christian apologists responded in one of two general ways to the new challenge: accommodating insofar as possible (as with John Tillotson) or by confrontation (as with William Law). John Tillotson, archbishop of Canterbury, argued that religious faith must be tested, accepted, and commended on rational grounds—making faith subject to reason. He also argued that the chief value of religious faith is to sanction morality, thereby minimizing the importance of distinctive Christian beliefs.

Tillotson attempted to make Christianity palatable to the modern world by drastically compromising its message. In attempting to make the gospel relevant, he promoted "contemporaneity" rather than "continuity" with the faith of the fathers.

William Law eventually entered the fray in opposition. He commented, "A revelation is to be received as coming from

God, not because of its internal excellence, or because we judge it to be worthy of God, but because God has declared it to be his, in a plain and undeniable manner, as he has declared creation and providence to be his."[5] We cannot bring God to the court of fallible human reason.

Law accented the transcendent character of God, the need of revelation not subject to human reason, and the latter as a corollary of the former. If we embrace the one, there is no reason to reject the other.

This separation has continued within Christian apologetics to the present. Some have stressed the compatibility of the faith to contemporary thought, while others have maintained its distinctiveness. The former has predominated in more liberal circles, the latter among the more conservative—with considerable variations in both camps.

The rise of the modern scientific movement added more fuel to the apologetic fire. Charles Darwin published *On the Origin of Species by Means of Natural Selection* in 1859. "It was a trumpet call which, if it did not demolish all the walls of security, at least tore great rents in them, and the winds of the new scientific age swept through disconcertingly."[6]

Darwin's evolutionary paradigm seemed to provide a plausible alternative to the previous theistic alternative. As a result, humankind was toppled from its exalted place in the biblical account. It appeared as little more than a complex form of animal life, derived from a common source and the result of thoroughly natural processes.

Samuel Wilberforce, bishop of Oxford, attempted to stem the naturalistic tide, but with little success. Theologian Charles Hodge managed better, pointing out the difficulties in Darwin's position, the limits of pure science, and the credibility of Christian faith. Here was a belated apologetic literature in the making, which would eventually provide the Christian with a firm place to stand in the scientific era.

A more recent illustration is found in Bernard Ramm's *The Christian View of Science and Scripture*. Ramm distinguished between "science" as a legitimate method of investigation and "scientism" as an unwarranted philosophic extrapolation. J. Edwin Orr (to the affirmative) and Michael Scriven (to the negative), in their debate concerning the credibility of Christianity, were in thorough agreement that "neither science nor any commonly held view of science contradicts belief in God."[7] Ramm concurred by stating as his purpose in writing: "There is nothing between the soul of the scientist and Jesus Christ but the disposition of the scientist himself."[8]

Ramm searched for a middle ground in his apologetic approach. The liberal, in Ramm's view, errs by limiting Scripture to its religious content, cutting short any dialogue with scientific data. The "hyper-orthodox" refuses to consider scientific data seriously. The unnamed middle option deliberately seeks to harmonize the teaching of Scripture with the legitimate insights of scientific investigation.

It is critical to Ramm's approach that he establish the nature of biblical language. He reasons that it is popular (the language of common people rather than some elitist alternative); phenomenal (as things would appear to an observer); non-postulational (neither prescientific nor scientific); and cultural (expressed in the idiom of the time).

Ramm dramatically concludes an extended inquiry into a variety of related topics: "We assert that a man may be a Christian without the sacrifice of his intelligence. To the contrary, we feel that Christian interpretation of man is the one which best accounts for the most facts."[9] The case for Christianity improves substantially when earnestly compared with the alternatives set forth.

The modern age has also been associated with humanism ("man is the measure of all things") and secularism (humankind and its activity provide the proper focus for life). Adherents have announced the demise of religious faith; if not in their time, then in the lifetime of their children or grandchildren. They have also had to recast their timetable about as many times as those who insist on setting the date for Christ's return.

As one person complained: "Let man build a roof over his head, and he thinks he has created the universe." So it has sometimes seemed with the current effort to manage alone, without God's counsel or enablement.

Christian apologists have come up with alternative explanations for the humanistic/secular phenomenon. Some saw secularism as an expression of human devolution, so graphically described in the opening chapter of Romans. Paul commented: "Instead of believing what they knew was the truth about God, they deliberately chose to believe lies. So they worshiped the things God made but not the Creator himself, who is to be praised forever" (Romans 1:25).

Others took what is essentially the opposite point of view. Harvey Cox, in his best-selling *The Secular City,* elected to celebrate the arrival of secularity as an invitation to assume human responsibility.[10] Rather than nostalgically recalling the good old days, he advocated that we press ahead with the exciting challenges of today.

No sooner had Cox profited from his insights than he began to have second thoughts. He expressed these in *The Feast of Fools,* in which he explained the relevancy of the sacred.[11] The hold of secularism seemed to be slipping.

What is the future for Christian apologetics? If consistent with the past, it will pass through periods of intense activity, followed by interims of relative neglect. It will sometimes anticipate the needs to be addressed, and on other occasions come up too late with too little. We can only hope that Christians of every generation and in every calling will take seriously the biblical mandate to communicate a carefully reasoned faith.

DISCUSSION QUESTIONS

1. What was the focus of Christian apologetics with the dawn of the Middle Ages? What conditions contributed to this approach?
2. What was the character of medieval Christendom? At what levels did medieval apologetics contribute to Christian awareness?
3. Discuss Anselm's argument for God's existence. What are its strengths and weaknesses?
4. In what contrasting ways did Christian apologetics respond to the Age of Reason? Illustrate how these options continue to be reflected to the present.
5. What problem does humanism/secularism pose for Christian apologetics? What are the respective merits of the various responses?

CHAPTER 5

Belief in God

I have a candidate for my favorite atheist: Michael Scriven, a well-respected philosopher. He appeals to me for several reasons: He is a disciplined scholar, reflects a genuine concern for his fellow humans, freely admits that he could be wrong, and recognizes how high the stakes are when they involve belief in God. If God exists, he concludes that the implications are awesome!

Scriven forthrightly declares that his major reasons for not believing in God are the inconclusive character of the arguments for his existence and the presence of suffering in the world. We will pick up on the first of these complaints in this chapter. The thrust of my response will be that (1) finite creatures must exercise faith in order to establish any comprehensive worldview; (2) probability arguments are pertinent in establishing a credible alternative and ought not to be given either too much or too little credit; and (3) such arguments appeal to people individually and collectively, given our internal disposition and external circumstances.

FAITH

Scriven might be described as an "evangelistic atheist." That is, not only is he a convinced atheist, but he thinks it important to persuade others to share his conviction. Once, in correspondence with him, I took issue with a comment from an earlier letter: "You say that you are an atheist, but atheism is what you don't believe (in the existence of God). What *do* you believe?" His response was conciliatory: "You are quite right. I don't believe in God, but I do believe in man. I am a humanist."

Some who deride belief in God fail to recognize that they exercise faith no less than the theist. Faith is the ingredient that makes a symbolic universe (worldview) possible. It is no less present in humanism than theism.

The Apostles' Creed begins pointedly with the confession "I believe." What distinguishes one's confession of it is not that he or she believes, but what follows as the content of the creed. Belief is not the monopoly of any person or group of people. It is a human characteristic, whereby we organize experience into some meaningful whole. We could not function at a human potential apart from the element of faith in our lives.

Even if it were possible to manage somehow without faith, contrary to my personal opinion, it would be at a level repugnant to our finer sensitivities. It would be to sink to the jungle code, where the strong prey on the weak. There would be no morality, no responsibility, no service, and no humanity as we understand it.

ALTERNATIVE FAITHS

There is such a thing as faith in faith itself. Imagine a loved one who is ill. We ask the attending physicians if he or she will get well. The doctors answer indirectly: "We have done all we can; all that remains is to have faith." Perhaps they feel the patient will die unless there is some remarkable, unexpected recovery, or they may have in mind the curative powers of faith.

We normally think of faith with reference to some object other than faith itself. In spite of all evidence to the contrary, humanists believe they can fashion for themselves and others an increasingly meaningful and fruitful existence. They are hard put to demonstrate that this is true, although they can introduce certain kinds of probability arguments to support their belief.

Some of us are much less optimistic concerning the perfectibility of humankind left to its own devices. Our successes seem more in the realm of technology than basic morality. The humanistic perspective seems to fly in the face of history, a position which if taken seriously would leave us even more vulnerable to the evil forces present in our world.

Religious faith can also prove to be our undoing, as the humanist is quick to point out. It has been said: "Man is as good as the gods he serves." This truth is evidenced in the rowdy gods of Olympus who did little to improve the moral fiber of ancient Greek society.

There are, of course, varieties of religious belief. We have polytheism, belief in a plurality of gods; pantheism, wherein God pervades the universe; henotheism, where one god is superior to all others and on whom they depend; and monotheism, the belief in one God. Orthodox Christianity is monotheistic in character and is the option upon which we will focus.

There is, in fact, some interesting correlation between the henotheistic notion of a high god and the monotheistic faith of Christianity. A friend and I were standing at the foot of a sacred tree in West Africa. Its giant, arching branches provided a holy canopy over our heads. Here the traditional priest would offer blood sacrifice to atone for sin and gain control over the evil spirits that were said to prowl the village by night.

The high god is common to West Africa. While known by the name assigned by the respective tribe, he is held to be the same deity. The high god is, by consensus, removed from everyday life and unpredictable in his actions. One is, as a rule, better off seeking the help of lesser divinities.

The rabbis had a provocative account of how the high god came to exist in human experience. They say that man continued to offend the Almighty in seven stages of decline, beginning in Eden and finishing with the oppression of the Hebrew children in Egypt. Each time, according to Talmudic thinking, God withdrew himself further and further, until at last he remained little more than a faded memory and an anonymous deity.

Traditional peoples often have alternative explanations that, nonetheless, show strong similarities. For instance, the Ashanti report that God tired of their matriarch pounding her pestle to prepare *fufu*—their traditional food. He decided to move up higher. Whereupon, the woman instructed her sons to gather mortars and pile them up so as to follow. When they ran out of construction material, she advised them to take the bottom mortar and place it on top—causing the whole tower to come tumbling down. Many were killed as a result, convincing the Ashanti to give up their presumptive efforts to follow God into the heavens.

The Christian believes that this transcendent deity, who alone is God, has taken the initiative to reveal himself in times past through the prophets and in these last days through his Son. Were it not for this divine initiative, we would likely still be worshiping at the sacred tree. We would be restricted to what Paul referred to as the time of people's ignorance (Acts 17:30).

There is a striking agreement in monotheistic circles as to what God is like if, in fact, he does exist. He would be sovereign—exceeding all others in power, knowledge, and goodness; independent of others; personal in that he acts, reflects on his actions, and relates to others as he chooses; not limited by time and space; and, properly understood, immutable. He would also be the creator and sustainer of life. It is with such a general consensus in mind that belief in God takes shape and the theistic arguments were formulated. Let's take a closer look now at these classic arguments.

TRADITIONAL ARGUMENTS

We noted earlier Aquinas's outstanding contribution to the classical arguments for God's existence. These have been refined by many others over the years. Here we will discuss only selective instances to get a hold on the arguments and their importance to theistic faith.

Aquinas argues that everything that happens has a cause, and this, in turn, has a cause, and so the series must be infinite or have a first cause—which we call "God." The argument is initially vulnerable at the point of excluding the alternative of infinite regression. The cause-effect perception may also be explained otherwise: as nothing more than statistical probability or as imposing human-structured thinking on observable sequences. Finally, there remains a great gulf between speculation concerning a "first cause" and the Christian concept of God as set forth in Scripture.

Consider a related line of reasoning. We know from the fact that there was a time when a thing did not exist, that it might not have existed at all or existed differently. Everything points beyond itself to something else. Hence, there must have been a time when nothing existed. In this case, nothing could have come to exist, for there was no causal agency. Since things came to exist, there must have been a noncontingent case, which we designate "God." While the argument here is better refined, the previous rebuttal still generally applies.

William Paley is credited for improving on the teleological argument from purposeful design. Paley was born in 1743 and educated in Giggleswick, England. He failed to apply himself, not only in his studies, but other ventures as well. Upon enrolling at Christ's College at Cambridge, Paley was almost always late for everything. Unless he had an early class, he characteristically slept until noon.

Then Paley was awakened at 5 A.M. one day by a fellow student, who informed him that he was a "fool" to be wasting his considerable gifts and opportunities. He was so struck by this unexpected visit that he lay in bed the greater part of the day, charting an alternative course of action. Thereupon, it was said that he never seemed to relax his academic pursuit, resulting in an impressive apologetic legacy.

Paley's teleological line of reasoning, as captured by John Hick, reads as follows: "It would be utterly implausible to attribute the formation and assembling of these metal parts into a functioning machine to the chance operation of such factors as wind and rain."[1] It follows that Creation is of a far more intricate design than a simple watch.

This brings to mind a classic passage from Alexander Pope's *Essay on Man:*

> Say first, of God above or man below,
> What can we reason but from what we know?
> Of man what see we but his station here
> From which to reason, or to which refer?
> 'Tis ours to trace him only in our own.

Paley pointed out that it would not weaken his argument if we had not previously seen a watch, if the watch worked imperfectly, or if we could not discover how some parts operated. While he hoped thereby to mute the critics, they replied in kind. Eighteenth-century philosopher David Hume *(Dialogue Concerning Natural Religion)* observed that we could expect order and adaptation within any relatively fixed environment. Moreover, he contended that the analogy was weak, seeing the universe does not closely resemble a vast machine. In any case, one could not infer from such evidence the existence of such a God as reported in Scripture.

Immanuel Kant (1724–1804) was more kindly disposed to the moral argument than the above. In his *Critique of Pure Reason,* Kant represented speculative reason capable of organizing sense experience but not dealing with divine reality. In his *Critique of Practical Reason,* he pointed out that the sense of moral obligation required that we postulate the existence of God, freedom, and immortality.

Kant argued first from inference from a moral order to a Divine Lawgiver. His assumption, while open to challenge, was that moral values are not genuinely capable of naturalistic explanation.

The second form of the argument is that anyone seriously committed to moral values implicitly recognizes a transcendent source, which we call "God." If by any other name, we still invoke deity.

The naturalist may respond by saying that moral codes simply evolve to suit the needs of society. We are driven to invent them so as to structure communal life.

Along a different line, critics point out that what Kant postulates concerning God falls far short of what Scripture reveals. If it demonstrates anything, it is of relatively little value.

Anselm's ontological argument remains the most tantalizing alternative for many. Often refuted, it comes back with renewed vigor. Anselm reasoned that God is a being than which nothing greater exists. Strictly speaking, his argument is valid only insofar as the human perception can be identified with God. Nonetheless, the widespread and persisting character of religious experience cannot be taken lightly. At some point, it seems more likely to assume God's existence than to seek to explain religious intuition otherwise.

C. Stephen Evans concludes: "Whether the arguments are rationally convincing to someone depends in each case on accepting some key premise or premises which are neither self-evident nor absolutely certain."[2] He, nevertheless, adds: "It would seem that such arguments, individually and collectively, could form a case for the reasonableness of theism, at least relative to its rivals."[3]

Kelly Clark cautiously admits: "Precious few of our beliefs in life can be or have been proved in the classical sense. Rather than be intimidated by the demand for classical proof, we should reinstitute the notion of proof or evidence as person-relative."[4] This suggests that evidence will be variously evaluated in connection with our unique experience of life. What is not convincing to one will appear significant to another. What seems inconclusive at one point in time appears to take on greater significance at another.

It may be less significant to reach consensus on some particular argument than to recognize their creative interplay in bringing people to faith. Borden Parker Bowne may have had something of this in mind when he was prone to say: "Theism is not explicit in anything, but implicit in everything."

The case for Christian theism fares best when compared with its rivals. Our choice is not whether to believe or not, but in what to believe. In whom or what are we to believe? Faith in faith? Faith in humanity? Faith in the quarrelsome gods of Olympus? The Christian alternative seems, by far, the most inviting.

Still, we need to add Aquinas's sage advice: "If the only way open to us for the knowledge of God were solely that of the reason, the human race would remain in the blackest shadows of ignorance."[5] Revelation provides the answer which reason can only anticipate. If there is a God, as the arguments would seem to imply, it would seem likely that he must take the initiative. Such is the Christian's understanding. The burden of proof, if such be insisted on, may not weigh so much on theists as on those who beg to differ from them.

Let's conclude with two examples that further illustrate what we have been discussing in theory. The first concerns a man who, as a youth, stood under a sturdy tree and called out: "If there is a God, let this tree fall and crush me!" He paused for a moment and then burst into laughter at the thought that he had disproved the existence of God. Some years later, he was in charge of some troops caught behind enemy lines. He mused within himself: "If I were wrong, I deserve nothing for myself, but please, God, help me get these men out of danger." The person involved was my homiletics professor in seminary.

The other relates to a longtime friend, who built a distinguished record as a clinical psychologist. Before his conversion, it seemed that people were asking him to dispense with reason by becoming a Christian. Then, one evening, he was invited to attend a lecture by an erudite young scholar, Edward John Carnell. He came away from the meeting convinced that he could use his mind in God's service and so gave his heart to the Lord.

Two people, variously disposed, searching for God—there are millions of such testimonies. The evidence is in; belief in

God is reasonable. I have often encouraged people that the Almighty is much more concerned to be found than we are in discovering him. Seek him; seek him with all your heart; seek him above everything else; seek him while there is still time.

DISCUSSION QUESTIONS

1. The issue is not whether we believe or not, but in what or whom we believe. Do you agree or disagree with the statement and for what reasons?

2. Review the theistic arguments. Which do you find most compelling? Compare your conclusion with others.

3. If you have used any of the traditional arguments with others, what was the result? How do you account for their response?

4. We noted earlier Bowne's comment: "Theism is not explicit in anything, but implicit in everything." What implications can you draw from his observation?

5. How do the stories of the homiletics professor and clinical psychologist illustrate the apologetic role of theistic arguments? How may the accounts illustrate the limitations of traditional reasoning?

CHAPTER 6

The Presence of Pain

MICHAEL Scriven, "my favorite atheist," volunteers a second reason for disbelieving in God: our experience of suffering. This is typically introduced as "the problem of pain," as in C. S. Lewis's book by that title.[1] This standard approach leaves something to be desired, as the following account may illustrate.

Alice Naumoff tells the story of her prized cat. It seems that the cat persisted in climbing up on the range, and Alice was afraid that the cat might be painfully burned. When she put the cat down, it reasoned: "My mistress does not allow me the freedom I want. How can I experience for myself what life is all about if she insists on inhibiting my experience?"

Finally, Alice decided that there was nothing to be done but allow the cat to experience for itself the danger involved. Thereupon, the cat questioned her owner's good intentions for allowing it to suffer a painful burn. From Alice's point of view, this constituted a no-win situation.

Alice further felt that her love for the cat ought not to have been in question, seeing that she had crawled out on a fire escape to rescue the frightened animal, which was an exceedingly difficult thing for Alice to do, because she has a dreadful fear of heights. (God, in analogous fashion, went out "on a fire escape" in the Crucifixion.)

We are left to reflect upon the story's implications. One thing seems initially certain: Suffering should be approached not as a separate concern, but as part of the larger life situation.

SPEAKING TO THE ISSUE

We, nonetheless, begin with Lewis's worst scenario on the topic: If God were loving, he presumably would not want his creatures to suffer. If he were omnipotent, as Christians claim, he would be able to protect them from suffering. Inasmuch as we experience pain, God must either not be compassionate or omnipotent or simply does not exist. Edgar Sheffield Brightman resolved this problem to his satisfaction by positing a finite god, who does the best he can and solicits our help. The orthodox Christian does not have this option and must meet the dilemma head-on.

Lewis wasted no time coming to the fallacy in this seeming impasse. When we confess God's omnipotence, we mean he can do anything within the scope of existing conditions or can alter conditions consistent with his righteous purpose. We do not mean that he can create a rock too heavy to lift or fashion a square circle. Nor would he act in contradiction to his moral nature.

According to Scripture, the circumstances are these: "For we are not fighting against people made of flesh and blood, but against the evil rulers and authorities of the unseen world, against those mighty powers of darkness who rule this world, and against wicked spirits in the heavenly realms" (Ephesians 6:12). We are at war!

I am reminded again of the grim realities of World War II, especially as they relate to the children caught up in the conflict. Sometimes their sullen faces and emaciated bodies continue to haunt me. Even so, we understood that suffering was endemic to military conflict.

I also recall God being graciously at work in our midst and with me in particular. He was asking the best of a bad thing. This is like so much of life in general, where a spiritual conflict of unimaginable proportions is being waged.

Lewis thinks the issue related to moral evil more prominent, although natural evil is more difficult to account for. Moral evil refers to what people do or neglect to do that adversely affects others; natural evil pertains to suffering caused by natural disasters—such as from storms, flooding, or drought. I would certainly agree that moral evil constitutes the much more prevalent cause for human suffering. However, natural evil may be just another aspect of a cosmos in agonizing conflict. Humans are caught up in a conflict that extends far beyond themselves, related to spiritual forces in heavenly places.

The cynic comments: "I could have created a better world than this." God did! He viewed the world he had created and declared that it was excellent in every way (Genesis 1:31). So it remained until sin entered in.

"You don't mean to imply that this is the best of all possible worlds?" the cynic replies. Given the circumstances, yes! God is working with the present situation in order to achieve his redemptive purpose. In the end, matters will be dramatically altered. For the present, he is said to limit the sins of the fathers to only the third or fourth generation, "but I lavish my love on those who love me and obey my commands, even for a thousand generations" (Exodus 20:6).

This reminds me of a rabbinic story. It seems that a cluster of observers were witnessing the flames devouring Jerusalem. All broke out in loud lament except one pious individual, who burst into joyous laughter. His companions were shocked and demanded to know why he rejoiced in the destruction of the

Holy City. The sage responded: "Because if the agony we now experience is so great, how much more will be our rejoicing when Jerusalem will be restored in the messianic age?" He sensed that the sufferings associated with this life anticipate rich dividends in the future.

We must not lose sight of the fact that God loves us, although we experience it in an adverse situation. Lewis positions God's love in the context of complex good; that is, as expressed toward and in a fallen world. This reminds me of a concern expressed by a former student, who was working as a nurse. She described an experience with a patient who kept crying out, "What have I done that God is punishing me like this?"

"What should I have said to her?" the pensive student inquired. I suggested, "Demonstrate that you care, perhaps by holding her hand for a moment. Later on, when she is better able to reflect on the matter, you can share your confidence in God's benevolent purposes." She smiled understandingly. We can remain either part of the problem or become part of God's solution. God will achieve his righteous purpose in any case. If we oppose him, we are still his tools; if we cooperate, he treats us as sons and daughters.

How may we assist? Lewis mentions two ways: (1) by accepting suffering, and (2) by repenting of evil. Suffering itself holds no merit. It is when we accept pain within the gracious purposes of God that we grow in spiritual maturity and learn how better to minister to others. This is the crux of the matter, as illustrated by the following:

I remember her well. She had suffered long and patiently. Her confidence in the Lord had not wavered for a moment. She seemed more concerned for those around her than for herself. She anticipated her homegoing. Her faith transformed pain into blessing, for herself and others.

As another case in point, a devout young couple was faced with a traumatic experience. They had looked forward with great anticipation to the birth of their first child, only to find it badly deformed. While the mother managed with difficulty to cope with the situation, her husband turned his back on God. Time passed. Eventually, they came to call the child their "love child," a precious gift of God that enhanced every aspect of their relationship together as a family.

We also contribute to God's redemptive strategy by repenting of our sin. While there may be few people who sin as grievously as King David, fewer still repent with such earnestness. We remember him not so much for his trespasses but for his contriteness of heart. He also bore witness to God's compassionate forgiveness and solicited his commendation of the Hebrew ruler.

"I don't believe she is a Christian," the deacon confided in me. "Why?" I asked. "Because of the things she says when angered," he maintained. "I suspect she is a Christian," I responded. "Why?" he wanted to know. "Because she so agonizingly repents when she does wrong." He was silent for a moment before acknowledging: "You may be right."

Genuine repentance assumes a commitment to change. If we have done that which we ought not to have done, let us desist from such behavior by the grace of God. If we have failed to do what we should have done, let us take up our responsibility through his enabling. Thus we cooperate with God in his benevolent design. As the formula now stands essentially complete:

Simple good
(God's unfailing expression of love, cf. James 1:17)
▼
results in complex good
(his love expressed toward and in a fallen world)
▼
to which accepted suffering and repented evil contribute.

VISITING WITH JOB

We can learn much from Job. "We generally treat the book of Job as a commentary on suffering, but it is much more than that. Pain certainly rushes to the forefront (both as physical affliction and mental anguish), but wisdom is the more persisting subject."[2] Job chronicles how a righteous man should deal with the vicissitudes of life, pain being a pressing concern among others.

Wisdom begins with "the fear of the Lord." Chuck Colson asks the rhetorical question: "What is most needed in the church today?" Many options might come to mind. He dramatically concludes: "It is the fear of God."

If we do not fear God, we will not heed his revelation. If we do not fear God, we will steer our own destructive course. If we do not fear God, society will pull apart. We begin to develop our life skills with the fear of the Lord.

"Where should I start?" The man was desperate for direction; his health was impaired by drug abuse, his wife had threatened to leave him, and he was in danger of losing his job. My advice was simple: "Get things straightened out with God. Then he will help you get the other matters in order. Leave God out, and you will struggle on your own."

Job's faith was severely tested. Yet, he reasoned: "I came naked from my mother's womb, and I will be stripped of everything when I die. The LORD gave me everything I had, and the LORD has taken it away. Praise the name of the LORD!" (1:21). Again put to the test, he responded: "Should we accept only good things from the hand of God and never anything bad?" (2:10). Such was the attitude commended by the biblical writer.

Job's fortunes were cast on a roller coaster. He had trusted God in plenty, he had to learn to trust him in want; he had trusted in health, he had to learn to trust in affliction; he had trusted when applauded by others; he had to learn to trust when ridiculed. All things work together for good for those who trust their ways to the Almighty (Romans 8:28).

Ambiguity is another important feature of the Job narrative. There is no precise correlation between a good life and material success. Motives are often obscure to both observers and to the individual. Simple answers do not satisfy complex life situations.

Take the case of a middle-aged woman who had left an established church to become involved in a predatory cult. "My minister would never give me an uncomplicated answer," she complained. It turned out that she was looking to escape from ambiguity and so had fled into unreality. However, a credible faith will help us live with uncertainty.

Tradition is another prominent theme in Job. Tradition is a legacy to be cherished. It represents the wisdom of past generations. To ignore tradition is to start from scratch.

Nevertheless, tradition ought not to be accepted uncritically. Times change, and with them change our way of response. We learn from the past in order to negotiate the present and anticipate the future. Tradition serves a constructive purpose, not as a crutch but as a catalyst.

There are many lessons that could be learned from faithful Job. We have mentioned several to illustrate that pain is best considered in a larger life context. We need to account not only for pain but pleasure, not only evil but goodness. If the theist must contend with the problem of *pain,* then the atheist must add the additional problem of *pleasure.* The latter has a much more difficult apologetic task.

VISITING WITH JESUS
Look at suffering over the shoulder of the Master. The German writer Helmut Thielicke, in his provocative work, *I*

Believe, pondered the nature of Christian faith in the light of human suffering. He imagined trying, in vain, to catch a glimpse of God through the mushroom cloud rising over Hiroshima. It was no use to remind him of the "God above the starry heavens." Faith had grown cold under the rain of ash covering the scarred earth and distorted bodies.

Thielicke identified more easily with the skeptic at this agonizing moment than with the complacent Christian. His was a troubled faith but, for that reason, more likely a genuine faith.

Did Thielicke believe in the God above the starry sky, secured from suffering below? No! He believed in the God revealed in Jesus Christ, who experienced rejection, affliction, and execution. He believed in the God who personally experienced pain.[3]

The Gospel of Luke records that Jesus was in anguish as he prayed in the Garden of Gethsemane and in anticipation of the Cross. "He prayed more fervently, and he was in such agony of spirit that his sweat fell to the ground like great drops of blood" (22:44). Newspaper columnist Jim Bishop speculates that this phenomenon resulted from Jesus' capillaries bursting from extreme anguish, exuding blood along with perspiration.[4] Whether correct or not, Bishop's explanation graphically suggests the extent of Jesus' suffering.

Jesus remained resolute. He staggered under the weight of the cross, having been weakened by a savage beating. He bore the pain of crucifixion, compounded by the scorn of those who passed by. He played the role of the suffering servant to a bitter and yet triumphant conclusion.

What are we to learn from Jesus' experience of suffering? The apostle Peter reasons that "since Christ suffered physical pain," we should approach pain "with the same attitude" (1 Peter 4:1). "So if you are suffering according to God's will, keep on doing what is right, and trust yourself to the God who made you, for he will never fail you" (1 Peter 4:19).

Paul takes the rationale a step further: "We can rejoice, too, when we run into problems and trials, for we know that they are good for us—they help us learn to endure. And endurance develops strength of character in us, and character strengthens our confident expectation of salvation" (Romans 5:3-4). Are we to rejoice in suffering? We don't glory in suffering as such, but in suffering that works perseverance and results in hope.

Do not seek suffering; seek rather to serve God. Should the latter entail suffering, accept it graciously. Know that pain can purge the spirit and further our Christian witness.

Pain remains for Scriven the one overwhelming obstacle against belief in God's existence. Yet, he wrote to me on one occasion that if he were to be convinced otherwise, it would most likely be through reflection on Jesus. This Galilean rabbi alone seemed to challenge his conclusions and make him think that he might be mistaken. Jesus aside, the obstacle of suffering seemed to this earnest philosopher, as to many others, overwhelming.

However, we have seen that the problem of pain does not refute Christianity. There are answers to this dilemma. In responding to the problem, we've added another plank in our developing case for believing in the Christian faith.

DISCUSSION QUESTIONS

1. Reflect on how other faiths approach the matter of suffering. For instance, Buddhism attempts to eliminate pain at its source by negating our desire for personal identity.
2. Is pain always an effective means for God to get our attention?
3. What are some of the lessons concerning suffering we can

learn from Job's experience? What was lacking in Job's defense of his integrity? What was missing in the counsel of his associates?

4. What experience have you had with suffering? Has it strengthened your faith, and, if so, in what ways?

5. Read John 9:1-3. What does this suggest for our understanding of life in general and suffering in particular?

CHAPTER 7

The Human Mystique

WHAT are mortals that you should think of us?" the psalmist exclaimed. "You made us only a little lower than God, and you crowned us with glory and honor. You put us in charge of everything you made, giving us authority over all things" (Psalm 8:4-6). Humankind was, according to Scripture, of noble origin and in a uniquely exalted position.

The subsequent devolution of humankind was graphically recorded by the apostle Paul: "Yes, they knew God, but they wouldn't worship him as God or even give him thanks. And they began to think up foolish ideas of what God was like. The result was that their minds became dark and confused" (Romans 1:21). Although they claimed to be wise, they became foolish—practicing idolatry rather than worshiping the living God.

In biblical perspective, one sees humankind as exhibiting an extraordinary capability, albeit misappropriated and misdirected. This might result in a peculiar mystique that would defy simplistic explanation. Let's look more closely at the human mystique.

CHARACTERISTICS

What is unique about humans? Four characteristics have been widely acknowledged: (1) complex symboling, (2) refined tool usage, (3) moral inclination, and (4) religious orientation. Complex symboling refers to a comprehensive use of language, such as to communicate about things far removed by space and time, abstractions, and projection of future events. No other creature appears to even approach the human mastery of symbols.

This and subsequent characteristics seem to fit the Genesis account of Adam and Eve. Not only do they speak, but speech appears as a corollary to their administration of creation. It was God's provision for them to fulfill their stewardship task.

Second, humans are similarly characterized by a refined use of tools. It is common knowledge that certain animals employ and even fashion tools for their use. For instance, a banana is placed just out of the reach of an enterprising chimpanzee. He picks up a section of a fishing pole, only to find that it is too short to reach the tempting fruit. He then joins one section with another in order to succeed in his enterprise.

Remarkable as this feat may seem, it is elementary when compared with the tool refinement that goes into a modern medical facility: the surgical instruments, diagnostic equipment, monitoring machines, and so on. The difference is so great that it deserves not simply to be thought of in terms of degree, but kind. Human refinement of tool assembly and use marks people off from all other creatures.

Third, the human moral inclination also appears to be distinctive. Our concern for right and wrong can take precedence over survival instinct or simple expediency, as in a newspaper account of two girls who had fallen into the Chicago River. A stranger leaped into the water to attempt a rescue and perished as a result. Why did he do it? One of his friends replied: "We had to try!"

Conversely, Victor Frankl probed the darker side of human nature with the dehumanizing effect of the extermination camps during World War II.[1] He separated his guards into three categories: those who attempted to make life as easy as possible for the prisoners, those who wanted no part in the inhumane treatment but cooperated, and those who seemed to enjoy inflicting abuse. Such is the range of human response we encounter from time to time.

Finally, humans are characterized by their religious disposition. Every so often one reads of some primitive tribe that appears not to be religious. Sooner or later, more times than not, a follow-up article admits a religious perspective not at first recognized. Religion among traditional people is so pervasive that it appears to be universal.

Moreover, modern secular humanity may not be as much an exception as we have been led to believe. Eugene Nida tells of sitting next to a man as they flew together over the sea of clouds spread out below. At one point the man inquired: "Do you really believe in God?" Although an elder in his church, he was uncertain. Was there anything to buttress his religious faith? Yes, he adamantly believed in ghosts, which were his bridge to the supernatural.[2]

The above four characteristics, each remarkable in itself, when taken together express something of the human mystique. The psalmist appropriately responds: "Thank you for making me so wonderfully complex! Your workmanship is marvelous—and how well I know it" (Psalm 139:14). Scripture adds, by way of counsel, that to whom much is given, more is required (Luke 12:48).

IN HISTORICAL PERSPECTIVE

Three keys have been advanced to establish human antiquity: biblical chronology, structural similarity, and artifacts. The first assumes that the Bible intends to provide a comprehensive chronology. With this in mind, a 4004 B.C. date was obtained for the creation of Adam and Eve.

Recent studies seem to suggest that traditional chronologies serve a variety of purposes, such as clan associations and memorable events, none of which require a comprehensive chronology. Perhaps the Bible is an exception, but evidence one way or the other seems lacking.

Structural similarity has been another clue advanced to identify the antiquity of humankind. The imprecision of this alternative can perhaps best be illustrated by sharing an experience. Along with several colleagues, I visited the Carmel excavations of Ofer Bar-Joseph, formerly of Hebrew University and now of Harvard University. He showed us a reproduction of his prized Neanderthal specimen, recovered from the base of a bone pit.

Neanderthal has been promoted as a near relative of Homo sapiens, and Bar-Joseph was quoted as saying that Neanderthal spoke as well as we do. Bar-Joseph repudiated this report, saying that we have no way of knowing whether the creature spoke at all, but there were structural similarities that suggested it could have approximated human language.

Bar-Joseph also challenged the concept that Homo sapiens descended from Neanderthal. His studies found that while the two overlapped in time, there was no evidence of association—let alone linkage between the two.

Cultural artifacts provide a final clue to human antiquity and are generally associated with Homo sapiens. We have in mind such things as cave paintings, refined flint blades, and stone vessels. These would clearly indicate a creature with a capacity quite similar to humans today.

At this point, some would reintroduce Neanderthal. Certain burial practices are thought to express a religious orientation. In particular, the inclusion of grave objects and border stones.

This data could be otherwise explained. To illustrate, I was asked to conduct a funeral service for a person unfamiliar to me. Upon entering the funeral parlor for the ceremony, I paused for a moment to gaze into the open casket. There, in the lapel pocket of the elderly man, was a vintage pipe.

I could have concluded from this that it had religious significance, but decided it was simply associated with the deceased and meant to be buried with him for that reason. The rudimentary grave objects of the Neanderthal might be accounted for along similar lines.

We may rest assured that the evidence is not all in on the subject of human origins. It seems best not to rush into a hasty and ill-advised dogmatism. Biblical revelation appears quite capable of vindicating itself, if the past has been any indication.

History, as we commonly employ the term, relates to what man has been doing more recently. John Warwick Montgomery has reviewed the perspectives of five prominent post-Enlightenment historiographers: Immanuel Kant, G. W. F. Hegel, Karl Marx, Oswald Spengler, and Arnold Toynbee. Kant and Hegel saw history as an escape to reason; Marx portrayed history as an inevitable economic drama; Spengler found no enduring progress, guiding spirit, nor ultimate goal—only endless repetition; and Toynbee declared that civilization fulfills its function when it brings to birth a more mature religion to chart the future. Montgomery finds little in common among these representative views of history and that set forth by Scripture.[3]

Biblical history, in a sense, begins with the exodus of the Hebrew people from Egypt. The Pentateuch reviews the course of history up to that time, details the events surrounding the Exodus, and sets the stage for what follows.

Never before or after has God selected an ethnic people, as such, to be his redemptive vessel. The situation was unique, and the Hebrew people would ponder from time to time why they had been chosen. Explicit reference is made to the righteousness of the patriarchs; beyond this, the reason lies within the inscrutable wisdom of God. One thing was certain: "Salvation comes through the Jews" (John 4:22).

Special instruction was necessary, seeing that the nations had fallen away from God. Israel went to the school of the prophets. It was a difficult course of study. They did not always get passing grades.

They, nevertheless, continued to hope, and their hope revolved around the promised Messiah. It was difficult to work the prophecies together into a consistent picture. Eventually, a Galilean teacher by the name of Jesus came on the scene. He began an itinerant ministry at about thirty years of age. It was accompanied by miracles. He showed compassion on the poor, infirm, and oppressed. His ministry struck a profound messianic note.

Jesus gathered a following, primarily at first from his own region of Galilee. Opposition grew steadily. Three years passed before the issue came to a head. Jesus challenged the commercial use of the temple, which was a special affront to the Sadducean authorities. He was apprehended, interrogated, and sentenced to death.

Something quite remarkable followed. It was reported that Jesus had been raised from the dead. His followers became bold with faith in the risen Lord and the indwelling Spirit. Their numbers multiplied rapidly. They diligently labored in anticipation of Jesus' return. So it has been to the present. The Christian account of history begins with reflection back on the

Creation, focuses on the redemptive act of Christ, and terminates with a sanctifying judgment at his return.

The Christian philosophy of history may be characterized as humanity's response to God's redemptive initiatives. In contrast, the post-Enlightenment perspectives leave little or no room for divine initiative. Humans are pretty much left up to their corporate efforts to carve out a good life, plagued by the memories of past failures.

ACCENT IN EVIL

The theme of tragedy is woven throughout human history and has been variously explained. For instance, Judaism developed a comprehensive view of the evil *yetzer* (inclination). The rabbis reasoned that one's evil *yetzer* grows ever stronger, seeking to destroy him or her. It at first resembles a spider's thread but eventually is like a rope of a ship. If God did not intervene, the person would succumb.

The evil inclination is, according to rabbinic teaching, something we can indulge in or not. If we once yield, the *yetzer* grows stronger. If we resist, by occupying ourselves with Torah, the *yetzer* will be unable to overcome us. We can never be secure from the evil inclination; pride comes before a fall. What tempts the evil person to fall purifies the righteous to holy resolve.

What impresses one with reading the rabbinic tradition on the evil *yetzer* is that it takes the tragic dimension of humans seriously. This is something often lacking in contemporary writers and lessens their credibility. A perspective not sensitive to human tragedy is likely not true; an alternative that takes tragedy seriously may be true.

The human tragedy is expressed both in individual and corporate manner. When theologians speak of "total depravity," they do not mean that everyone is as bad as they could be. They rather mean that the sinful nature is pervasive; there is no aspect of human nature left untouched as the result of sin.

I was once asked to lecture at a federated church, which drew together divergent theological traditions. When I mentioned "sin," some took offense. "We don't believe in sin," they explained. A brief interchange followed. They allowed that people do "evil," for which they should repent. Thereafter, I was careful to describe evil as the Bible would interpret sin. Everyone seemed quite satisfied.

We distinguish between sins of commission and omission. The latter are probably, in most instances, more offensive than the former. In any case, humans are remarkably creative in the way they can give vent to their evil disposition.

The Christian believes that sin basically constitutes an affront to God. Others may be and regularly are affected, but this is not the primary focus. The psalmist concluded: "Against you, and you alone, have I sinned; I have done what is evil in your sight" (Psalm 51:4).

Evil is also deeply rooted in institutional life. We socialize our privilege, neglect, and oppression. We bear a corporate guilt before the Almighty. We further compound our guilt with religious hypocrisy.

A person once confided in me: "I can't believe in God because of people's evil ways." Conversely, that is one reason I am encouraged to believe. Scripture tells it like it is—tragedy and all.

Our review of the human mystique has strengthened our argument for Christianity. In the next chapter we will consider the human longing for immortality and its implications for our case.

DISCUSSION QUESTIONS

1. What is implied by the account that humans were created in the image of God (Genesis 1:27)? How may this be related to the human characteristics discussed above?

2. C. S. Lewis suggests that it is more important for apologetic purposes that people have a sense of right and wrong than that there is a consensus on what is right or wrong. Do you think his point is well taken? Explain your answer.

3. Which of the three options for determining human antiquity seems most plausible? What are sources from which we may gather new evidence?

4. Bodie Thoene, in her novel *Jerusalem Interlude,* has the Mother Superior of the Russian Orthodox convent that borders on the Garden of Gethsemane observe: "We mortals have a small and troubled view of time, Samuel. If the wicked could have one glimpse of their eternal future, perhaps they would repent. And if the righteous could have one glimpse of their eternity with God, they would no longer fear what evil men might do to them in this life." How might her comment bear on the present topic?

5. Reflect on the claim: "If God is dead, man is also dead." What might this imply for the importance of the human mystique for Christian apologetics?

CHAPTER 8

In Search of Immortality

WHAT would it mean to live forever? One of the most persisting beliefs of humankind from antiquity has been with regard to an afterlife. Artifacts found buried with the departed were meant to equip them for the life to come. The Egyptians succeeded in preserving the deceased's body to accommodate the future life. Ancient texts describe in vivid detail events thought to transpire once one had passed on. There has been a near universal hope, even if not confidence, that life survives death.

While immortality and the resurrection are not precisely the same thing, they are closely associated. Were it possible to establish the former beyond a reasonable doubt, the latter would appear much more plausible. There is much at stake in this connection: "For if there is no resurrection of the dead, then Christ has not been raised either. And if Christ was not raised, then all our preaching is useless, and your trust in God is useless" (1 Corinthians 15:13-14).

PHILOSOPHIC ARGUMENTS

Warren Young lists a series of philosophic arguments given in support of immortality. The first is based on the distinction between soul and body. He observes: "Some kind of distinction between physical body and immaterial or semi-immaterial soul seems to be as old as human culture."[1] Plato argued that while the body belongs to the sensate world and shares in its changing nature, the intellect is associated with the realm of universal ideas and changeless realities. As he succinctly put it in *Phaedo:* "The seen is the changing, the unseen is the unchanging."[2]

It has been further claimed that human nature is of such value as to necessitate its perpetuation. I was never more impressed with the logic of this viewpoint as when asked to participate in the burial service of my paternal grandfather. He had been a devout person, whose piety carried over into a disciplined, earnest, and industrious lifestyle. It seemed incredible to think that all this could come to such an abrupt and permanent termination. I felt compelled to account for his life in terms of its contribution to those still living, with regard to the afterlife, or a combination of the two.

It may be human potential that implies immortality. This is the direction C. S. Lewis's thinking takes in *Mere Christianity.*[3] He reasons that if we have an appetite, it presupposes a means to satisfy it; if we have a sex drive, it likewise presupposes a means whereby it can be satisfied. However, if we experience a hope which nothing in life satiates, then we are left with several possibilities. We may conclude that hope is related to childish fantasy; it is something to be put away as we mature. Or we may decide that circumstances have robbed us of fulfillment: the failure of parents, lack of appreciation from our employer, or choice of an insensitive spouse. There is finally the Christian option: If there is nothing in this life which corresponds to hope, as food to hunger or sex to the sexual drive, then hope is most likely associated with an unfulfilled potential in the future life.

Our belief in immortality is confirmed by analogy. The classic case for immortality by way of analogy was presented by the eighteenth-century author Joseph Butler. Butler was born in 1692, raised in a Christian family, studied law, and eventually was ordained. His substantive work *The Analogy of Religion* (1736) was a Christian apologetic against the rampant deism of the time.

Butler suggests that immortality resembles the sowing of a seed in the ground, which generates life in the springtime. It also resembles the metamorphosis of a caterpillar into a butterfly. Probability, according to Butler, provides the ground for belief, and analogy gives us direction. Immortality is thus said to be consistent with the pattern of life as we experience it, without which the order we observe would break down.

Our present existence would be, at best, incomplete and even unjust if there were no future life. How else can we account for the fact that the good suffer, and evil people escape retribution? How else can we understand that some die in infancy and others are severely retarded? If anything remains to be completed, and if there is any semblance of justice, it would seem to require life after death.

Humans rise to the challenge of their unique existence as drawn by hope in the future life. It is hope that cultivates concern for their vocation and fellow human beings. It is hope that keeps them from degenerating to the code of survival of the fittest. Humans are less driven by their past than drawn by their anticipated future, a future beyond the grave.

While we may put greater or lesser importance in one line of reasoning or another, the impact of the sum is greater still—just as a rope is stronger than its individual strands. At the very least, they illustrate the seriousness with which people consider the probability of life after death, in that they construct elaborate arguments in its defense. It may well be that the arguments reflect an abiding and correct perception that future life exists, even though they, when taken individually or even collectively, are not altogether persuasive.

RELIGIOUS ARGUMENTS

Young turns our attention from philosophic to religious considerations. Immortality is often represented as a component of religious faith. It is an intricate part of some larger religious system. It could not be removed without doing serious damage to the rest.

Immortality may also be promoted on the basis of quantitative testimony. It is widely believed in various faiths that life survives death. It is not a narrowly confined religious conviction that might otherwise be written off with a flourish. It also persists in the face of atheistic propaganda, cruel oppression, and painful disillusionment with institutional religion.

A wide range of unlikely examples comes to mind. There was a young physician indoctrinated into atheistic communism. She had no church affiliation. She had no Bible nor portion thereof. She, nonetheless, seemed compelled by some inner reflection to believe in the existence of God (however understood) and immortality. She was only one person among many, each with his or her own unique witness to faith in immortality.

Immortality may be a subject of revelation. It is, as such, either a direct teaching or related to some other dogma. Paul asserts that our earthly bodies must be transformed into heavenly bodies that cannot perish but will live forever (1 Corinthians 15:53). At that time, death will be swallowed up in victory. He states this confidently, as a matter of record.

Belief in immortality may also appear as a spin-off of some other teaching. If, for instance, people are to be held accountable, and life does not afford the opportunity for justice to be administered, a future life would seem called for. Some extension of life, if not immortality per se, would seem to be the necessary corollary to accountability. As often stated: "He will get what is coming to him." If not sooner, then later on.

DIRECT EXPERIENCE

We still need to consider the experiences of those who claim personal contact with life after death. The first form this testimony takes is in connection with those reported to have been clinically dead and returned to life. There are striking similarities in many of the reports. For instance, those involved often sense having been in a lighted area and seeing relatives and friends. They likewise experience a reluctance to return to life as they have known it.

While a wide range of discrepancies in the accounts could lead to skepticism, their frequency and some general consensus might argue for credibility. We need, in any case, to bear in mind that these people are only clinically dead, whose vital organs are still capable of functioning. The experiences may have little or nothing to do with life after the body deteriorates beyond recovery.

The second form of direct evidence is related to the alleged conversation with departed spirits. This is the reason for which spiritualism exists. The Hebrew was strictly warned against such practice, which was associated in the prophet's thinking with idolatry and demonism. But if it were possible to be in contact with a departed spirit, it would certainly conclusively demonstrate life after death.

"Would you like to know your future?" inquired a medium. I answered in the negative. She seemed genuinely disappointed. She professed to have a contact in the spirit world, who would provide information on request.

Short of actual confirmation, such matters as we have introduced provide cumulative evidence for immortality. At some point, it becomes more likely than not. The balance tips toward the affirmative.

IMMORTALITY OR RESURRECTION?

The Christian believes beyond immortality in the resurrection. Theologian Krister Stendahl has given classic expression to this differentiation: "I put the death of Socrates and the death of Jesus side by side. For nothing shows better the radical difference between the Greek doctrine of the immortality of the soul and the Christian doctrine of resurrection. . . . [Jesus] cannot obtain this victory by simply living on as an immortal soul, thus fundamentally not dying. He can conquer death only by actually dying."[4]

The notion of resurrection grows out of the Hebraic concept of the unitary nature of humankind. It does not share in the radical soul/body dichotomy developed in Greek thought. It was not until Paul turned to the resurrection of the dead that his Athenian audience began to deride him (Acts 17:32). This conflicted sharply with their philosophic orientation.

Paul, nevertheless, concluded:

> It is the same way for the resurrection of the dead. Our earthly bodies, which die and decay, will be different when they are resurrected, for they will never die. Our bodies now disappoint us, but when they are raised, they will be full of glory. They are weak now, but when they are raised, they will be full of power. They are natural human bodies now, but when they are raised, they will be spiritual bodies. For just as there are natural bodies, so also there are spiritual bodies. (1 Corinthians 15:42-44)

As we have borne the image of the earthly, so shall we bear the image of the heavenly.

Immortality and resurrection contrast in other ways. Stendahl comments, "Belief in the immortality of the soul is not belief in a revolutionary event. Immortality, in fact, is only a negative assertion: the soul does not die, but simply lives on. Resurrection is a positive assertion: the whole man, who has really died, is recalled to life by a new act of creation by God."[5]

Yet the contrast between the Greek idea of the immortality of the soul and the Christian belief in the resurrection runs still deeper. The belief in the resurrection presupposes the Jewish connection between death and sin. "Death is not something natural, willed by God, as in the thought of the Greek philosophers, it is rather something unnatural, abnormal, opposed to God."[6] Death is a curse; it is the mortal enemy of humans.

Immortality and resurrection, therefore, view the human dilemma differently. Socrates welcomed death as deliverance from the inhibition of life in the flesh. His was a beautiful death, accompanied by reassuring platitudes. Jesus agonized at the approach of death, resolute in obedience to his Father's will, and eventually triumphed over sin and death. Sin is the problem, death the cruel adversary, and Jesus' resurrection the indication of dramatic victory.

These contrasting beliefs foster quite different attitudes. Again Stendahl observes:

> The emperor Marcus Aurelius, the philosopher who belongs with Socrates to the noble figures of antiquity, also perceived the contrast. As is well known, he had the deepest contempt for Christianity. . . . [It] was just the martyrs' death with which he was least sympathetic. The Stoic departed this life dispassionately; the Christian martyr on the other hand died with spirited passion for the cause of Christ, because he knew that by doing so he stood within a powerfully redemptive process.[7]

Let's take the contrast one step beyond Stendahl's carefully argued treatise. Faith in immortality is speculative unless one takes at face value the reports of those who are said to return from the dead or have communication with the departed. Faith in the resurrection rests on the earnest of Christ's resurrection. "But the fact is that Christ has been raised from the dead. He has become the first of a great harvest of those who will be raised to life again" (1 Corinthians 15:20). After the firstfruits, we can anticipate the full harvest.

While the case for immortality paves the way for faith in resurrection, the Resurrection confirms the prospect of future life. When asked to read an appropriate passage at my grandfather's grave, I proclaimed not philosophic argument or theological extrapolation or personal experience, but Christ's triumph over the grave.

That is not all. As Stendahl so vigorously argued, belief in the resurrection from the dead is a redemptive and revolutionary faith that makes the immortality alternative pale in comparison. It confidently affirms that Christ has triumphed over sin and death, that the power which raised Jesus from the dead now indwells those who believe, and that the general resurrection will, in due time, come to pass.

We have looked closely at the "human side" of the case for Christianity; we will now, in the next chapter, examine in more detail the divine side—the historical Jesus.

DISCUSSION QUESTIONS

1. What value do you assess to the testimonials of those said to have been clinically dead? What significance do you give to the reports of communication with the departed?

2. Read 1 Samuel 28 in connection with the appearance of Samuel to Saul. What do you make of this unique biblical instance, especially in light of the prophets' prohibition against consulting mediums?

3. Stendahl suggests: "If we were to ask an ordinary Christian today what he conceives to be the New Testament teaching concerning the fate of man after death, with few exceptions we should get the answer: 'The immortality of the soul.'" What implications might this have for Christian apologetics?

4. How might the Christian apologist approach the resurrection of Christ in a traditional culture where a person's recovery from death is thought not altogether uncommon?

5. Read the account of Paul's Athenian address (Acts 17:16-34), especially in regard to his audience's reaction to the announcement of Jesus' resurrection. How does this illustrate the contrasting points of view as elaborated by Stendahl?

CHAPTER 9

The Quest for the Historical Jesus

ESUS comforted his disciples with the words: "You trust God, now trust in me" (John 14:1). They were not only the beneficiaries of revelation in nature and conscience, but of the prophets. What more could be desired? Trust also in Jesus: take a calculated step from prophetic to Christian theism.

In order to do so, we must wend our way back nearly two thousand years to unfamiliar surroundings and events that altered the course of history. We must take up the quest for the historical Jesus to uncover the roots of the Christian faith. It bears repeating: The Christian faith is not so much a faith in something than in Someone.

JESUS OF NAZARETH

"Jesus" was a common name. The Jewish historian Josephus mentions about twenty people by that name, ten of whom were contemporaries of Jesus of Nazareth. The name means "Yahweh helps, delivers, or saves." Perhaps more striking, certainly less obvious, was the anticipation that the Messiah would, along with a select few Old Testament people, be named before birth.

Scripture has little to say about Jesus' early years. The

apocryphal work *Infancy* describes him forming a bird from clay and breathing life into it. On another occasion, he was reported to have miraculously altered a length of board which Joseph had incorrectly measured. These were simply pious attempts to fill in what was lacking in the biblical record.

Luke wasted no words in summarizing Jesus' maturation: "Jesus grew both in height and in wisdom, and he was loved by God and by all who knew him" (Luke 2:52). Wisdom is "knowledge aptly applied." Thus, we may conclude that Jesus developed physically, intellectually, socially, and religiously.

Chaim Potok, in his novel *Davita's Harp*, tells of a puzzling interchange between Davita and her mother concerning the account of Herod's massacre of the children. "And King Herod was Jewish," Davita said. "So was Jesus," her mother replied. "Jesus was Jewish? Aunt Sarah never told me that," Davita exclaimed.[1] Jesus was certainly Jewish. He identified with the Jewish people, their legacy, and their mission.

He was also Galilean. Jesus was, from the perspective of the Judeans, "a stupid fellow," because his speech seemed less refined and less pleasing to the ear. Then, too, as was generally assumed, if one wanted to be wise, go south to Judea.

The Galileans were a feisty lot. They were accustomed to defending what they thought to be right. Gamala and the cliffs of the Arbel provided natural defense positions for the Zealots. Galileans were considered either freedom fighters or troublemakers, depending on one's perspective. Whatever Jesus' personal character, this was the stock from which he came.

Jesus grew up in a devout Jewish home, which was the center of religious life for his people. Here he received basic instruction in the Jewish faith. We also know that there was a synagogue in Nazareth and that it was Jesus' custom to attend its services. We do not know how far he may have progressed in formal education. A branch of the Via Maris (Way of the Sea) trade route ran just the other side of the ridge from Nazareth, likely bringing Jesus into early contact with strangers from distant lands.

Jesus appears to have been strong of build, as would be supposed from his vocation, stamina, and incidental references. He had a commanding presence. He, likewise, exhibited extraordinary sensitivity and compassion. It may have been his "human" qualities that first appealed to people: He was obviously humanity at its very best.

JESUS THE TEACHER

"The crowds were amazed at his teaching, for he taught as one who had real authority—quite unlike the teachers of religious law" (Matthew 7:28-29). It was not what he said, as impressive as this may have been, but the way in which he said it. He set aside legal precedent with the formula: "You have heard that it was said . . . but I tell you." In our modern thought, it was as if he constituted a new "paradigm" around which they were to understand divine revelation.

His miracles attested to the truthfulness of his teaching. He touched the body, and it was made well; he commanded the blind to see, and they saw; he ordered the winds and waves to be still, and they obeyed. "Who is this?" the disciples inquired among themselves. "Even the wind and waves obey him!" (Matthew 8:27).

They also noted that Jesus assumed divine prerogatives as a matter of course. Once, when they had brought a paralytic to be healed, Jesus declared, "Take heart, son! Your sins are forgiven" (Matthew 9:2). Some who were present thought to themselves: "Blasphemy!" (9:3). Knowing their thoughts, Jesus declared that he had spoken in this manner so that they might know that he had "authority on earth to forgive sins" (9:6).

On another occasion, his opposition inquired: "Are you greater than our father Abraham?" (John 8:53). He responded in such a way as to solicit again the charge of blasphemy by applying to himself the theophany formula "I am!"—recalling Moses' encounter with God in the burning bush (Exodus 3:14).

Jesus' claim was both in keeping with traditional Jewish thinking and yet radically new. Hebraic monotheism was complex in character: God was said to reside in heaven, but could also reveal himself in some other connection—such as the burning bush or with the Angel of the Lord. Novelty aside, Jesus' announcement was consistent with the Hebrew mind-set.

It was also a radical messianic departure. Previous manifestations of God (theophanies) were passive in character, while the Incarnation was active. Ethelbert Stauffer elaborates: "It was the profoundest declaration. God himself had become man, more human than any other man in the wide expanse of history."[2] Astonishing as this might seem, everything else now fit into place in the light of this remarkable revelation.

This reminds me of an experience from the disestablishment sixties. I had been asked to lead a Bible study in an inner-city coffeehouse. As I looked at the circle of people seated on the floor, one person especially intrigued me. His hair fell long on all sides so as to muffle his speech. As a result, he had cultivated the habit of throwing his head first to one side and then the other, so as to articulate more intelligibly.

We were discussing a Gospel passage concerning Jesus when he alerted us of his intent to comment by shaking his head. We all paused. "Man," he exclaimed with regard to Jesus, "God was all there!" I have never heard it stated quite that way in any theological text, but we all heartily agreed with him.

A CONTINUING QUEST

For some faiths, history is inconsequential. It does not really matter much whether Buddha actually lived or not; the Buddha (enlightenment) is within. Not so with the Christian faith. It is inexorably tied up with its founder.

Yet, times change, and with them our way of looking at Jesus. Our view is influenced by the assumptions of the age in which we live and to what degree we accept those premises as true. John Reumann writes in the preface to Joachim Jeremias's *The Problem of the Historical Jesus:* "It makes a profound difference whether one approaches this prophet who died upon a cross from the standpoint of medieval piety, or the Reformation principle of 'grace alone,' or the lordship of reason, or the nineteenth century's optimism about the world and man, or the twentieth century's more pessimistic existentialism."[3]

Professor Reumann identifies three stages to the continuing quest for the historical Jesus: the old quest, no biography (Christ of faith), and the new quest—all related to the modern era. The classic example of the nineteenth century's old quest was Ernest Renan's *Life of Jesus.* It reflected the rise of rationalism and the advent of critical textual studies.

Renan portrayed Jesus' ministry in rustic fashion:

> The faithful band led thus a joyous and wandering life, gathering the inspirations of the master in their first bloom. An innocent doubt was sometimes raised, a question slightly skeptical; but Jesus, with a smile or a look, silenced the objection. At each step—in the passing cloud, the germinating seed, the ripening corn—they saw the sign of the kingdom drawing nigh, they believed themselves on the eve of seeing God, of being masters of

the world; tears were turned into joy; it was the advent upon earth of universal consolation.[4]

This phase in Jesus' teaching quickly passes. Jesus is contaminated by contact with others. His mind is gripped with apocalyptic terrors. He becomes incriminatory and vindictive.

Still, Renan's Jesus rides out the turbulence of life. Renan concludes with magnanimous praise (given his naturalistic bias):

> Mankind in its totality offers an assemblage of low beings, selfish, and superior to the animal only in that its selfishness is more reflective. From the mind-set of this uniform mediocrity there are pillars that rise towards the sky, and bear witness to a nobler destiny. Jesus is the highest of these pillars which show to man whence he comes, and whether he ought to tend. In him was condensed all that is good and elevated in our nature.[5]

Renan adds that Jesus was not without sin, nor was he ministered to by angels or tempted by Satan. Likely, he imagines that both virtues and faults were concealed by the biblical writers.

The problems with the "old quest" are legion. It took unacceptable liberties with the biblical text in order to fit with preconceived impressions; it imposed a rationalistic mentality alien to the Bible; it dismissed the biblical writers as ignorant primitives; it reconstructed Jesus to fit a particular author's preference; it resulted in innumerable lives of Jesus, substantially different from one another and often inconsistent within themselves. The well ran dry for the old quest and its once zealous adherents.

The pendulum swung from the Jesus of history to the Christ

of faith. Rudolph Bultmann took center stage with his *Jesus and the Word* (1925). Bultmann's theological understanding drew upon his ministry to people physically and emotionally scarred from war. They needed an infusion of the faith of the early Christians in order to face life courageously and make the most of their limited opportunities.

Bultmann's remedy can be seen in the following: "God is God of the present, because His claim confronts man in the present moment, and He is at the same time God of the future, because He gives man freedom for the present instant of decision, and sets before him as the future which is opened to him by his decision, condemnation or mercy."[6] The Christ of faith, stripped of the antiquated mythology of the New Testament, becomes the crux of the biblical message.

Bultmann soon came under attack by his former students. The Christ of faith, void of the Jesus of history, had no objective character, no reason for being, and no credibility. The "no biography" approach had understandably reacted against the follies of the old quest, without realizing the implications of the proposed alternative.

Once again the pendulum swung, not back to the presumptive extremes of the old quest, but toward a more moderate position. Gunther Bornkamm's thinking is representative: "The nature of the sources does not permit us to paint a biographical picture of the life of Jesus against the background of the history of his people and his age. Nevertheless, what these sources do yield as regards the personality and career of Jesus is not negligible, and demands careful attention."[7] In particular, students of the "new quest" asserted that we could know, at the very least, the basic outline of Jesus' life and teaching. We may, in fact, know considerably more, but it is better that we practice restraint—given the excesses of the former quest.

This is approximately where the quest for the historical Jesus stands today. An occasional exception makes an appearance, like a shooting star seen for the moment but soon gone. The new quest appears to retain its credibility, at least for the present, and probably for some time to come.

We return to Ethelbert Stauffer for some closing comments. Stauffer was a contemporary to Bultmann, advocating what he termed a "historical approach" to Scripture. He argued that the historical approach makes use of sources to determine what transpired. If in conflict, so much the better, because it helps us get a fix on the point at issue.

For instance, was Jesus known to have performed miracles? His disciples say yes, and so do his opponents, who admit the miracles by attributing them to satanic power. Bultmann might reply that this was simply a primitive mythology asserting itself by seeing miracles in outstanding people. Stauffer anticipates this move by reminding his readers that there was an outstanding contemporary of Jesus to whom miracles were never attributed, that is, John the Baptist.

The crux of the issue for Stauffer was Jesus' claim concerning himself. Did he really claim to be the messianic theophany of God, very God and very man? So his disciples reported, and with this the opposition agrees by entering the charge of blasphemy. For Stauffer, this is bedrock historical fact.

Where does this line of reasoning leave us? We must reach a decision, as did those who heard Jesus speak. We may charge him with blasphemy, or we may own him as Lord, but it is virtually impossible to find a credible option between.

Was Jesus mistaken? He would seem to be the most insightful of people; one would not think him easily misled. Was he purposely attempting to mislead others? (Renan is driven to this conclusion with reference to Jesus' "hoax" of raising

Lazarus from the dead.) This would seem blatantly unethical. Was he misunderstood? It appears not.

The most viable alternative left to us would seem to be that he is who he claimed to be. If Jesus is God, we've discovered foundational evidence for making a case for our cause. However, our quest for the historical Jesus can take us no further. The Bible must be the next point in our investigation.

DISCUSSION QUESTIONS

1. How would you answer a person who says that we can know nothing of Jesus because the Gospel writers were biased? Are they consistent in carrying over their skepticism to other ancient sources?

2. Why is it unwise to divorce the Christ of faith from the Jesus of history? What becomes of the Christ of faith void of the Jesus of history and vice versa?

3. When can a simple reading of the biblical text be the best apologetic approach? When may something else be called for?

4. How would you account for the discrepancy between the guileless life of Jesus and the less-than-exemplary life of so many who profess to follow him? Consider the effect of the discrepancy for Christian apologetics.

5. Are we to think of Jesus as a great religious leader, one among others, or the unique Messiah of God? Have we other options? Which seems the more likely and for what reasons?

CHAPTER 10

The Bible and Truth

IF the Bible is true, the Christian faith stands validated. If false, in any regard, this will be considered a strike against Christianity. The truthfulness of Scripture is obviously an important consideration for any study of Christian apologetics.

The issue naturally begins with the claim of Scripture concerning itself: "No prophecy in Scripture ever came from the prophets themselves or because they wanted to prophesy. It was the Holy Spirit who moved the prophets to speak from God" (2 Peter 1:20-21). "All Scripture is inspired by God and is useful to teach us what is true and to make us realize what is wrong in our lives. It straightens us out and teaches us to do what is right" (2 Timothy 3:16). God was said to have employed human authors to convey his infallible Word.

Exploring the Issue

An author may state what he or she thinks to be true without it actually being true. To accept biblical veracity solely on the basis of its own witness appears to some as circular reasoning. Critics remind us that we normally do not accept a claim as true without corroborating evidence.

Evidence can be of two varieties: internal and external. There is much within Scripture that lends credence to its authorial claim. We will touch on four considerations: (1) authorial preference, (2) uniformity of witness, (3) miracles in general, and (4) prophecy in particular.

First, it has been customary, following Aristotle, for historical and literary scholarship to give the benefit of doubt to the author rather than critic. The clear expression of the author ought to be considered valid unless disqualified by internal contradiction or known inaccuracies.

While considerable effort has gone into disproving the Bible, the results have, for the most part, been unimpressive. The core of problems are minuscule, the bulk of problems manufactured. I recall a seminary professor waving his Greek New Testament around his head with the challenge: "I could reduce the real problems to a page and a half of the Greek text, and, for this reason, who would argue that I surrender my confidence in the veracity of the biblical text?" No one took issue with him; his case seemed compelling.

Second, the Bible is a collection of works compiled over a span of sixteen hundred years, involving more than forty authors, reflecting a stated or generally implied consensus concerning the character of Scripture. Some years ago, H. H. Rowley reflected back on his liberal theological training. It had emphasized at every turn the diversity of Scripture. Rowley had come to realize that diversity was only one side of the coin; there was also a remarkable unity to take into consideration. Wherever one starts, Rowley concluded, whether with diversity or unity, he or she is obligated to consider the other. It was for him a matter of professional competence.

The consistency of the Bible witness is here at stake. The critic must not only overturn the witness of a solitary writer, but that of a resolute tradition.

Third, there are the authenticating miracles recorded in Scripture. These cannot be easily written off as the product of a prescientific era. There is a restrained character to biblical miracles that distinguishes them from other ancient sources. They occur, as C. S. Lewis reminds us in *Miracles,* not randomly, but cluster around critical points in divine revelation.

Where miracle is the order of the day, it loses any leverage as a means of verification. It is rather when the miraculous appears in some meaningful context or another that we are impressed by its relevance. Such is the persistent and obvious pattern of the biblical account.

Fourth, prophecies deserve our special consideration. Peter forthrightly declared: "But God was fulfilling what all the prophets had declared about the Messiah beforehand—that he must suffer all these things" (Acts 3:18). Paul further elaborated: "I passed on to you what was most important and what had also been passed on to me—that Christ died for our sins, just as the Scriptures said. He was buried, and he was raised from the dead on the third day, as the Scriptures said" (1 Corinthians 15:3-4). The Bible speaks with one voice concerning the fulfillment of prophecy in the coming of Christ.

Prophetic fulfillment is not related to few isolated instances but is at the core of the proclamation of the early Christian community. We cannot remove it without creating havoc with the message. It remained for the earliest Christians a continuing witness to the veracity of Scripture.

We ought also to consider as external evidence historical corroboration, preservation of the text, canonical considerations, and the transforming power of the biblical message. William Albright, renowned archaeologist, subsequently wrote: "The excessive skepticism shown toward the Bible by important historical schools of the eighteenth and nineteenth centuries has been progressively discredited. Discovery after discovery has established the accuracy of innumerable details, and has brought increased recognition to the value of the Bible as a source of history."[1]

For instance, the Hittites were once unknown to secular history and thought by some critics to be mythical people. Archaeology has subsequently uncovered the remains of a significant Hittite nation, which was able to challenge the armies of Ramses II. This was not a small accomplishment for a people once thought to be nonexistent.

Even so, the critic is correct in pointing out that historical accuracy does not necessarily validate biblical inspiration. It is what we would expect if the Bible is inspired of God. But one cannot say that because we found an inscription concerning Pilate that, therefore, the Bible is uniformly trustworthy, much less divinely inspired.

John Warwick Montgomery aptly concludes: "To be skeptical of the resultant text of the New Testament books is to allow all of classical antiquity to slip into obscurity, for no documents of the ancient period are so well attested bibliographically as the New Testament."[2] The comment could readily be extended to the Old Testament as well. The sheer bulk of manuscript evidence is staggering; the results of textual reconstruction are singularly impressive. The biblical text has been preserved like no other work of antiquity.

This fact suggests, if nothing else, the genuine uniqueness of Scripture. It has been preserved, at great personal cost, as God's Word for succeeding generations. No comparable regard has been shown for any other work.

It has likewise been preserved as the standard (canon) of truth. The early church fathers were careful to distinguish between their writings and those of the apostles as represented in the biblical text. They wrote to inspire, but not under divine inspiration. Tradition was intended to clarify biblical teaching, not supplement it, and certainly not to contradict it.

It was not the task of the early church to decide but to recognize which books deserved to be included in the canon. Those included were thought to be of divine origin, authoritative in all matters of faith and practice. They constituted the corporate witness of the Christian community to the prophetic refrain: "Thus God says."

No work has had such a profound and lasting impact on history as the Bible. It has transformed both individuals and societies. Biblical references punctuate world literature. Such results cry out for an explanation as persuasive as it being the inspired Word of God.

How powerful is it? I knew a missionary who told of leaving a Gospel portion in a remote tribe some years earlier. Upon returning, he was surprised to find a flourishing church fellowship and believers who had already begun an outreach to surrounding villages. This is only one of countless accounts of the impact of Scripture on the lives of those who ponder its message.

It does not substantially harm the argument to point out that some people have misappropriated Scripture for selfish ends. This might be expected. They will be judged by the standard they choose to pervert.

However, the cumulative effect of the above considerations ought not to be taken lightly. Nevertheless, we must turn to another kind of consideration, one which seems to have special apologetic merit. We'll now examine Jesus' own testimony concerning the trustworthiness of Scripture.

JESUS' WITNESS
The (liberal) modernist, early in the century, liked to pit the teachings of Jesus (red-letter version of the New Testament) against the rest of Scripture. It did not work then, nor does it

work better now. Jesus directs us to Scripture, even as Scripture returns us to Jesus.

John Stott introduced a public lecture on biblical authority some years ago at a Wheaton College chapel with the rhetorical question: "Why do we believe the Bible to be the infallible Word of God?" The answer was for him really quite simple: "Because Jesus did and taught that we should." Biblical truthfulness is not some evangelical peculiarity, but normative Christian faith.

The charge of circular reasoning disappears in this approach to biblical authenticity. All one must initially do is to recognize, along with the prevailing attitude of the new quest, that we have recorded in Scripture at least the basic outline of Jesus' life and teaching. Once confronted with the claims of Jesus, we may choose to accept or reject them. If we accept them, then we need to press on to embrace his teaching on Scripture, as we would his teaching on other matters.

Let's look at the place of Scripture in Jesus' life, teaching, controversies, and relative to his messianic calling. When tempted to turn stones to bread, Jesus responded with the words: "The Scriptures say"; when urged to cast himself down from the pinnacle of the temple, he replied: "The Scriptures also say"; when offered the kingdoms of this world if he would worship Satan, he maintained: "The Scriptures say." Each time he insisted on abiding by the revealed Word of God (see Matthew 4:1-11).

Jesus announced his intent to live by the precepts of Scripture. He deliberately strove to accomplish this purpose. He never wavered, regardless of opposition, discouragement, or cost involved.

He also taught others to live according to the Scriptures. "Don't misunderstand why I have come. I did not come to abolish the law of Moses or the writings of the prophets. No,

I came to fulfill them" (Matthew 5:17). "How terrible it will be for you teachers of religious law and you Pharisees. Hypocrites! For you are careful to tithe even the tiniest part of your income, but you ignore the important things of the law—justice, mercy, and faith. You should tithe, yes, but you should not leave undone the more important things" (Matthew 23:23).

Jesus made it clear that he understood the essence of the Torah was to love God thoroughly and our neighbor as ourselves. These were the chief concerns of Scripture, the essence of sacred teaching, the course Jesus set out for his disciples, and the standard he held up for others. One could not listen long to Jesus without being directed to the Torah.

Scripture was also Jesus' final court of appeal. He complained:

> And why do you, by your traditions, violate the direct commandments of God? For instance, God says, "Honor your father and mother," and "Anyone who speaks evil of father or mother must be put to death." But you say, "You don't need to honor your parents by caring for their needs if you give the money to God instead." And so, by your own tradition, you nullify the direct commandment of God. (Matthew 15:3-6)

We ought not to employ tradition to circumvent the Scripture. Our disputes ought to be settled, not with appeal to fallible tradition, but infallible Scripture.

Where Scripture speaks, we should affirm. Where Scripture does not speak, we should be cautious. We ought neither to lag behind nor rush ahead of biblical revelation.

Jesus finally alluded to Scripture in the context of his messianic calling. When apprehended, he responded: "I was there [in the Temple] teaching every day. But these things are happening to fulfill what the Scriptures say about me" (Mark 14:49). As the revealed Word of God, these things must come to pass.

Thus, Jesus entered his passion as a biblical mandate. If possible, he wished to be spared the agony, but obedience to the will of God was paramount. He died as he had lived—by the Word of God.

Jesus' "Bible" was, of course, what we refer to as the "Old Testament." There could not have been an "Old Testament" at the time, for there was no "New Testament." The case for biblical authority as related to the New Testament must be constructed differently: by way of anticipation, apostolic office, witness of miracles, and acceptance. Jesus observed that he had much more to say to his disciples, but they were not presently able to bear it. But in due time the Holy Spirit would guide them into all truth, equip them for their mission, and sustain them in their endeavor.

The disciples had reason to expect that the teachings of Jesus, refined with the coming of the Holy Spirit, would result in an extension of Scripture. It would be a matter of recording what had, to that point in time, been oral communication. They would not be left to accomplish this on their own but could expect the intervention of the Holy Spirit as implied by Jesus' promise.

The promise of guidance into all truth was especially relevant for the apostles. The Mishnah (a collection of Jewish oral tradition) affirms that the word of the *shaliach* (emissary) is as the one who sends him. The word of the apostle was to be understood as originating with Christ.

Such seems to have been the apostles' understanding of the matter. Paul appropriately comments: "Now, about the young women who are not yet married. I do not have a command from the Lord for them. But the Lord in his kindness has given me wisdom that can be trusted, and I will share it with you" (1 Corinthians 7:25). Paul makes these observations in the larger context of his apostolic office (chapters 4 and 9), suggesting that they relate to the *shaliach* tradition. His rigorous defense in Galatians should also be understood primarily as zeal over the apostolic office, rather than personal vindication.

All but a few miracles recorded in Acts were in connection with the apostles. These are apparently meant to be signs authenticating the apostolic office. They are divine approval of the vocation of Christ's emissaries and to gain a proper hearing.

As a case in point, Peter and John were approaching the temple at the season of prayer (Acts 3). A crippled beggar sat by the gate asking for alms. Peter fixed his eyes on him and spoke: "I don't have any money for you. But I'll give you what I have. In the name of Jesus Christ of Nazareth, get up and walk!" (3:6). The beggar leaped to his feet; the people were amazed; the apostles were given opportunity to speak on behalf of Christ.

Further, the Christian community accepted the apostles as ambassadors of Christ with *shaliach* credentials. Their message came to be associated with the New Testament, so that Scripture came to embody "the law, prophets, and apostles." Peter pointedly comments: "Some of his [Paul's] comments are hard to understand, and those who are ignorant and unstable have twisted his letters around to mean something quite different from what he meant, just as they do the other parts of Scripture—and the result is disaster for them" (2 Peter 3:16). While we cannot determine for certain whether Peter uses the reference to "Scriptures" in a technical sense, it seems in keeping with the understanding of the early church.

Thus, we conclude that both Old and New Testaments

ought to be understood as the inspired Word of God, as verified by Jesus' testimony. Such a view should not be considered a sectarian idiosyncrasy, but a settled Christian conviction.

Stott concluded his lecture with a needed admonition: If the Bible is indeed the inspired Word of God, we ought to cherish it; if it is the Word of God, we ought to diligently study it; if it is the Word of God, we ought to obey it; if it is the Word of God, we ought to share its message with others.

Is the Bible true? The evidence seems compelling. If Scripture is true, we've added another important piece in our developing case for Christianity. Next, we'll turn to an examination of miracles and see what testimony such signs have to offer in authenticating the Christian faith.

DISCUSSION QUESTIONS

1. Why is accepting the biblical claim to truthfulness at face value open to the charge of circular reasoning? How does recourse to Jesus' witness escape this criticism?
2. Review the internal evidence for biblical inspiration. Are there other aspects that might be added?
3. Review the external evidences for biblical inspiration. How can you enlarge on the points mentioned?
4. Reconsider Jesus' approach to the Old Testament. What additional biblical references have a bearing on this topic?
5. Martin Luther was reported to have said that the Bible resembles a roaring lion that only needs to be set free. This might imply that no apologetic is required with regard to Scripture. In what sense might this be true and in what sense not?

CHAPTER 11

The Significance of Signs

JESUS was a miracle worker! This is the clear testimony of the Gospels. Why miracles? The apostle John appears to confirm that signs (miracles) authenticate faith with the comment: "Jesus' disciples saw him do many other miraculous signs besides the ones recorded in this book. But these are written so that you may believe that Jesus is the Messiah, the Son of God, and that by believing in him you will have life" (John 20:30-31).

People are not nearly as ready to accept signs as evidence today. As philosophical descendants of the eighteenth-century Enlightenment emphasis on rationalism, we continue to hold a dim view of the miraculous. Rather than accepting miracles as authenticating signs, many see them as a holdover from a more primitive era. All this creates a new challenge for the Christian apologist.

MODERN ERA

Scottish philosopher David Hume (1711–1776) is perhaps the best-known critic of miracles. He launched a devastating attack against the credibility of supernatural events. He defined miracle as a "transgression of a law of nature by a particular volition of the Deity, or by the interposition of some invisible agent."[1] It can be readily seen that this definition presupposed a mechanistic view of the universe, subsequently altered by Albert Einstein's theory of relativity. It also failed to take into consideration the larger context of biblical miracles as special revelatory events.

Definition aside, Hume focused his attack on witnesses to the miraculous. He suggested that they were usually (1) uneducated; (2) fell prey to the temptation to believe in the exotic and strange; and, (3) as partisan religious adherents, offset one another.

First, Hume's "educated person" clearly reveals the disposition of those tied into his own skeptical tradition. He displays little patience with the sage of the past or those outside his own rationalistic Enlightenment tradition.

Shifting course, Jesus observed: "I tell you the truth, it is very hard for a rich person to get into the Kingdom of Heaven. I say it again—it is easier for a camel to go through the eye of a needle than for a rich person to enter the Kingdom of God!" (Matthew 19:23-24). Perhaps this would apply not only to those with an abundance of material possessions, but those with accumulated knowledge as well.

As a case in point, I vividly recall the self-assured grin on a university professor. "Once upon a time I used to believe in God and miracles," he acknowledged, "but no longer." He had, to his way of thinking, matured beyond the need of a religious faith, to the acclaim of his academic peers and the delight of many of his supportive students.

Second, Hume is reluctant to admit that the belief in things thought strange may suggest that life has a supernatural quality. But what if there are unseen spirits? We might be vaguely aware of their presence without being able to focus clearly. Our inclination is at least no better evidence against a reality than in its favor.

There is more substance to Hume's final criticism. It would at first seem that the conflicting witness of religious partisans might offset one another. Not necessarily! Scripture reports that there is a general revelation available to all, even though distorted by the course of time and events. If so, conflicting reports may still appear as corroborating evidence for the miraculous.

For example, I remember a group experience while mountain climbing. We had pressed on to the summit in spite of the threat of a gathering storm. As we reached the spur that extended down from the plateau, the storm broke in all its fury. Partway along the spur, there was a crash of thunder and flash of lightening. The three people with me were thrown to the ground, and one lay dazed. Afterward, we compared our varying impressions. Each had an unique account of an experience shared to some degree in common. Such might be the case with differing reports of our encounter with the miraculous.

Hume finally insisted that frequency be applied as a test to reported miracles. We have confidence in what can be repeated time and again under prime conditions.

This is true enough, but miracles, by their nature, do not fit readily into this pattern. They are, as a rule, distinctive occurrences, related to divine initiative, and primarily related to critical junctures in progressive revelation. They are not the kind of matters that can be reproduced at will.

They may, nonetheless, occur. For instance, we have evidence that meteorites do infrequently strike the earth, even though we would have difficulty predicting when this will occur. They are exceptional events, each unique in itself, but established beyond any reasonable doubt.

Some are now, in fact, predicting that the earth will be hit with a formidable asteroid before the year 2040. They claim there is enough circumstantial evidence to justify such a claim. They also think that they can predict, with some degree of accuracy, the nature, and, to a lesser degree, the extent of damage. This may prove a more proper analogy for miracles than the frequency criterion.

Hume and his associates also tended to overlook what transpires in the wake of miracles. I was eating lunch one day at the university cafeteria, when one of my classmates stopped by. I clearly recall his testimony: "My parents did not believe in the Resurrection, neither did the pastor of my church believe, nor have my seminary professors. Yet, I have come to believe that Jesus was raised from the dead. Why? Simply because it is the most plausible explanation for the existence of the church." My friend had expressed confidence in a miracle on the basis of observed results.

JEWISH CONTEXT

Biblical signs occur primarily in a Jewish setting. Thus, it seems proper to inquire into the traditional Jewish understanding of miracle. A casual reading of Jewish sources reveals the following: God may choose the miraculous as a means of accomplishing his purpose; this does not preclude human responsibility, neither does it presume that God will select a miraculous intervention; and we should, in any case, exercise faith in an all-sufficient and compassionate deity.

We ought not rule out what God in his creativity may choose to employ. He may decide to reveal his power and will in some extraordinary fashion. He has done so in the past; we can never eliminate the possibility he will do so again and again.

Consider the case of a young Indonesian with the novel name of "Bang-Bang." I asked Bang-Bang whether he had become a Christian through contact with a missionary or national. "Neither," he replied with a shy grin. "Then, through reading the Scripture?" I inquired. "No, not through anything read," he replied. He then confided how Jesus had come to him in a dream, saying to him: "Bang-Bang, I have chosen you to be my messenger to your people." He was at the time a graduate student in South Korea, training to serve in his calling—as the result of a miraculous intervention.

We ought not, nevertheless, sit back and expect God to work. Jewish writers have been quick to point out the importance of medical research and practice. Whether God chooses to heal by way of human instrument or through miraculous intervention is up to him. Ultimately, it is God who heals, whatever the means.

A friend of mine was to have surgery. As the medical staff wheeled him into the operating room, he demanded that they pause while he offered prayer. Thereafter, he petitioned along this line: "Dear God, you know how limited these people are in their abilities and skills. I commend the oversight of this surgery to you, without whom there can be no healing." With this, he announced: "I'm ready whenever you are." Having been reminded of their marked limitations and thorough dependency on the Almighty, the surgeon and his associates proceeded with the task at hand.

To state the Jewish ideal differently: Act as if everything depends on you; trust as if it depends solely on God.

Talmudic writers hasten to add that we should not put ourselves "in the way of miracles." That is, we should not presume on God. If a truck is bearing down on you, jump out of the way! When encouraged to leap from the pinnacle of the temple, Jesus replied in good Jewish fashion: "Do not test the Lord your God" (Matthew 4:7).

God, in his good wisdom, works differently with each of us.

Francis Schaeffer recalled how he had covenanted with God never to reveal the financial needs of his ministry. This was not to convince himself, but others, of God's unfailing faithfulness. He never recommended the practice to others, nor criticized those who took an alternative approach.

All of life should be lived to the glory of God and for our enrichment. We eat from his table what he provides. Signs may or may not be part of our fare. It really does not matter, so long as our confidence rests firmly in him.

There was a zealous young man who reported visions of Jesus. He seemed to feel that this somehow enhanced his spirituality. This was debatable. It could have just as readily suggested his dire need. The important thing was not whether he had visions of Jesus, but whether he was walking with him.

SPECIAL CASES

We now come to consider two special kinds of signs/miracles: biblical prophecy and the Resurrection.

Regarding prophecy, the late A. Berkeley Mickelsen warns of two erroneous approaches: (1) that which denies the existence of prophecy; and (2) treating prophecy as history beforehand.[2] The former approach was fostered by Bible critics. They assumed that prophecy does not happen and, therefore, did not happen.

How, then, did they account for biblical prophecy? Either the prophecy was of such general nature that it could have been "fulfilled" in countless ways, or it was written after the event. Some entertained the idea that people actually set out to fulfill prophecy on their own. Hugh Schonfield's highly speculative *The Passover Plot* is a prime case in point. Still others pointed out the existence of prophecy in extrabiblical sources as a cause of embarrassment.

Admittedly, some biblical prophecies are of general nature: The Messiah would be born of a woman, so are people as a rule; he would be born in Bethlehem, not a large village, but births there were not infrequent; he would enter Jerusalem on a donkey's colt, as do many, even to the present.

However, many prophecies are not so easily disposed of, nor is their cumulative effect. Daniel's account of the rise and fall of succeeding empires was so precise as to lead skeptics to insist it must have been written at a later date. His chronology concerning the coming of Christ appears on target. No late dating can altogether account for so remarkable a set of occurrences. Then, too, we are not dealing with isolated prophecies but a composite. As I once put it: "The prophets fashioned a sandal which only fit Jesus' foot perfectly."

As to dating the books of the Bible, this should be done on accepted historical-literary grounds. They should not be given a late date simply to accommodate a naturalistic bias or an early date merely to accommodate a conservative preference. We ought rather to weigh all the pertinent evidence available.

Josh McDowell reminds us that many of the prophecies concerning the Messiah could not have been purposefully enacted. Among these he mentions the place of birth, time of birth, manner of birth, betrayal, manner of death, people's reactions, piercing, and burial.[3] McDowell concludes that whereby certain messianic prophecies could be tied to other historical figures, sixty "major prophecies" were fulfilled in Jesus.

I inquired on a former occasion: "What do you think about when the subject of prophecy is mentioned? A gypsy fortune-teller, bent over her crystal ball, peering into the future? An elaborate wall chart, marked in contrasting colors, detailing events of the last times? These images mislead us into thinking prophecy is primarily concerned with revealing future events."[4] Rather, in fact, it is concerned with divine disclosure. The embarrassment connected with prophecies such as those of Nostradamus and Jeanne Dixon is not that they duplicate biblical prophecy, but that they may be thought to seriously resemble it.

Second, we can err conversely by treating prophecy as history recorded before the event, as evidenced by a plague of sensationalistic literature on the topic. This alternative assumes too much and is too quick to identify prophecy with current events. Mickelsen reminds us that history requires the circumstances into which the prophetic data fits. You are not there until you arrive!

Prophecy was not meant to satisfy idle curiosity, foster pride in esoteric doctrine, or divide believers into hostile parties. It was intended to console the oppressed, warn the fallen, and set our aspirations on things to come. Its apologetic value is not so much in isolated events that come to pass, as impressive as these sometimes may appear, but in the course of history as it runs true to revealed expectations.

The Resurrection constitutes another special case of miracle. Bernard Ramm reached four fundamental conclusions concerning Jesus' resurrection: It was the personal miracle of the Messiah, a major cog in the plan of redemption, the seal of our impending resurrection, and of significant evidential value.[5] While John details a number of miracles in his Gospel, the Resurrection comes as a climax. There ought to be no doubt concerning Jesus' messianic credentials, seeing that he was raised from the dead!

Paul concurs that Jesus "was shown to be the Son of God when God powerfully raised him from the dead by means of the Holy Spirit" (Romans 1:4). He was vindicated over his enemies, raised to the place of authority, and now intercedes on behalf of the faithful.

The apostle also observes: "He was handed over to die because of our sins, and he was raised from the dead to make us right with God" (Romans 4:25). Without the Resurrection there would be no offer of salvation. Because he lives, we are delivered from death to life. Because he lives, we may enjoy life eternal.

The revival of Lazarus did not guarantee life after death. His resurrection ended in death; Jesus revived to life evermore. As Paul predicts: "There is an order to this resurrection: Christ was raised first; then when Christ comes back, all his people will be raised" (1 Corinthians 15:23).

As noted earlier, the Resurrection serves as prime Christian evidence. The same person who had been rejected, ridiculed, and crucified God has raised, honored, and empowered.

The Resurrection, likewise, gave evidence that the redemptive program was on track. What Jesus had set out to accomplish would be completed in due time. The climactic victory had been won; the opposition continues to struggle in a losing cause. As penned by an anonymous author: "He is Lord, he is Lord! He is risen from the dead and he is Lord! Every knee shall bow, every tongue confess that Jesus Christ is Lord!"

Signs and miracles exist; they clearly point to another— Jesus Christ. His resurrection is the greatest miracle of all. It truly is, as Josh McDowell has penned, "evidence that demands a verdict."

DISCUSSION QUESTIONS

1. How has the Enlightenment impacted the evidential value of signs (miracles)? How does this alter the approach for Christian apologists?
2. A doctoral student once defined miracle as "any truly

creative human enterprise." How does this differ from a biblical perspective on miracles?

3. A person showed me a picture of the Virgin Mary, which was said to exude oil from time to time, as a miraculous evidence. How do you react to this type of alleged miracle? For what reasons?

4. It has often been said that Christianity stands or falls with the Resurrection. Do you concur?

5. Of the world faiths, only Christianity claims an empty tomb. What do you make of this unique phenomenon?

CHAPTER 12

Christianity and Religion

THERE once was a time when most Americans could grow up without ever coming directly into contact with an advocate of any religion but Christianity. As the cultural makeup of our nation has changed, it has become increasingly difficult to do so. The world has been shrunk to the size of our TV screen. Now, the family next door does not simply go to a different church, but may be Muslim or Hindu immigrants.

The apologetic problem this awareness of religious pluralism creates is not the lack of faith, but its variety. How are Christians to understand the world religions knocking at their front door? How does this affect our conviction that Jesus is the way, the truth, and the life? Let's take a closer look at the interplay between Christianity and other world religions by examining what others have to say about the subject.

MODEL #1

Sir Norman Anderson introduces three ways in which other religions may be viewed: as a preparation for Christianity, as satanic confusion, and as the result of human endeavor.[1] We are again reminded of Paul's address to the Athenians: "God overlooked people's former ignorance about these things, but now he commands everyone everywhere to turn away from idols and turn to him" (Acts 17:30). He stops short of representing other religions as actual preparation, even though he treats them as such.

So-called "redemptive analogies" abound in religious practice, as we observed earlier in connection with the apologetics of Justin Martyr. For instance, those familiar with blood sacrifice in religious settings may find the Crucifixion readily compatible with their former beliefs.

Prior religious conditioning can also work adversely. I recall a man who staunchly defended the religious validity of traditional religions over against Christianity, even though he professed to be a Christian. One got the impression that we could do without Jesus, seeing there had been godly people before and after him.

Those akin to this person's point of view see God's providential hand at work in all world religions. These religions are portrayed as way stations in the journey of faith. They are partial truths, or truths seen partially.

Others take the opposite point of view. They treat world religions as the devil's lie, meant to turn people away from divine revelation. Religion, thus understood, becomes the ultimate human weapon against the Word of God.

Tommy Titcomb, veteran West African missionary, tells a story of his encounter with traditional religion. It seems that he was returning from a Bible study with village Christians and came across an ecstatic company of natives gyrating to the urgent beat of drums. In the midst of the circle was a young girl levitating. Titcomb, incensed that Satan should demonstrate such power, pushed his way through the crowd and took hold of the young person. It felt as if a strong current passed through his body, and he was thrown back against a tree—much to the amusement of those who witnessed the event.

Titcomb reflected on the need of prayer in preparation for spiritual conflict, by which time the meeting had drawn to a close. He later found the girl recovered from her experience and led her to faith in Jesus. Such was the negative context in which Titcomb viewed rival faiths to Christianity.

The third option advocates that world religions result from human efforts to approach God. They are simply the product of mixed motivation, both good and bad. Their results are likewise mixed, except in that they fail to take into consideration the divine initiative.

Much that passes as "religious dialogue" partakes of this point of view. Each participating faith may be acknowledged as a legitimate human aspiration for the Almighty. Any truth that may exist is most likely to be found in consensus. As one of my university professors put it: "I never feel closer to God than when involved in some vigorous debate."

From where do rival faiths come? From God, Satan, humanity, or some combination? Probably a combination, but we will continue to accent one source over the others. Moreover, our choice will profoundly affect our apologetic approach to those of rival religious convictions.

MODEL #2

Thomas Owen takes a more detailed approach to the topic. He categorizes the ways in which Christians have viewed world religions as common core, spiritual values, internalization, variant perspectives, evolution, progressive revelation, and revelation/sin.[2] Some suggest that the world religions believe in the existence of God (however conceived), immortality (however different), and morality (with regard to basic principles). These are said to provide a common core of religious beliefs among Christians and those of other faiths. By implication, what is distinctive to Christianity is incidental and perhaps even counterproductive.

This position is difficult to sustain. I once encountered an Asian student, who inquired about one of my classes. My course unit was on world religions and, at the moment, focused on Buddhism. He countered that Buddhism is fundamentally atheistic and ought not to be thought of in religious terms—in spite of the religious devotion connected with it. His point may be contested, but what we often assume as common in alternative faiths is, upon careful review, quite diverse.

Granted that the common-essence option seems strained upon close scrutiny, let's turn to the spiritual values alternative. It is not religious beliefs, as such, that we hold in common, but the lifestyle they foster. Both Jews and Christians teach that we must not bear false witness against our neighbor; Hindus affirm that a lie voids the effectiveness of sacrifice; and Chinese sages urge us to keep our promises. Veracity is a virtue for them all.

Ethics, no matter how important a consideration, is not the totality of a religious faith. Moreover, ethical codes vary considerably. The cow is sacred to the Hindu, but to few others; a Buddhist monk immersed in flames as a voluntary protest is abhorrent to both Jews and Christians; even what constitutes proper behavior within religious traditions may differ substantially.

Unimpressed by the above options, some have turned to internalization as the common feature of religion. Some years ago a friendly rabbi observed, "I think you have something in your emphasis on the need of a new birth. Every faith has to internalize itself." He may not have grasped what Christians mean by the new birth, or simply chose to ignore it in favor of his novel interpretation.

If this is all that religious faiths have in common, it is not much with which to concern ourselves. It seems to imply that there is nothing more than religious psychology for common ground.

There is a still more popular alternative: that religious truth be viewed from divergent perspectives. The often repeated Indian story concerning the blind men who come upon an elephant demonstrates this point well. One takes the elephant by the tail and determines that it resembles a snake. Another grasps it by a leg and concludes that it stands like a tree. Still another feels its side and decides that it resembles a wall. Each, in his turn, reports truth from his particular perspective.

A university professor was similarly inclined when he drew a pie on the board and sliced it into pieces. "Each of these resemble the faith of a particular religion," he concluded. "Christianity is simply one piece among others." I looked to see if one was drawn larger than another. There seemed to be no difference.

Truth seems hopelessly fragmented by such an approach. We might do better to speak of religious "relevance" than "truth." Divine initiative appears most notable by its absence.

The evolutionary paradigm is also introduced here as a means of explanation. It is aggressively argued that religion was evolved from primitive animism, through faith in tribal gods, to the high monotheism of the Hebrew prophets and Christianity. The inferior religions remain as vestiges of the past, faiths that have not given way to a more mature form.

The evidence is capable of various interpretations. For instance, it might suggest that polytheism is an erosion of a primitive monotheism. Perhaps we would do better to think in terms of devolution than evolution. Otherwise, religions still suspiciously manipulate the evolutionary ladder to arrive at their own particular variation.

My general criticism of the above options is that they do injustice to the unique character of the Christian faith. What Christianity holds in common with world religions may be a proper apologetic concern, but it must be balanced over against Christian particularism. Owen's final two categories do better in this latter regard.

Progressive revelation (the process of God revealing himself in the Bible) may superficially appear similar to the evolutionary alternative, but not upon closer scrutiny. Progressive revelation posits a God outside the historical process; evolution provides an internal, naturalistic life force. With progressive revelation the eyes of the Lord search all around the world (Zechariah 4:10); evolution is blind process.

Progressive revelation resembles the way parents train their children. They employ the events that their children encounter as a means of instruction: an insight here, another there, now a little, then more, as the child is able to grasp the truth unfolding.

The good news for world religions in the context of progressive revelation is that they may embody truth in the process of being refined. The bad news is that they may represent premature closure. They resist the final stages of God's redemptive revelation.

The final prism through which Christians have viewed world religions is revelation/sin. "From the time the world was created, people have seen the earth and sky and all that God made. They can clearly see his invisible qualities—his eternal power and divine nature. So they have no excuse whatsoever for not knowing God" (Romans 1:20). Since the foundation of the world, the invisible God has been clearly expressed through his person and might.

On the other hand, sin intervened. Humankind refused to honor God or to offer him praise. It became increasingly corrupted, not only doing evil, but taking pleasure in the depravity of others. God, therefore, surrendered them to their evil lusts, and they became confirmed in their ways. The revelation/sin motif resonates well with biblical teaching.

LOOSE ENDS

Not all faiths fall precisely into the same category from a Christian perspective. There are the natural religions, such as Hinduism and Buddhism. These seem an effort to put together a religious system based solely on general revelation. They tend to obscure, in the process, recollections of the high god, such as with the Chinese Shangti tradition.

These natural religions do not seem to differ fundamentally from what Paul encountered in Athens. The apostle noted their religious zeal, confusion of worship, and reference to the high god. He further declared that they should turn to God at the hearing of the gospel, as attested to by the Resurrection.

I inquired of a Buddhist priest if many Americans were embracing his faith. "Few on religious grounds," he replied. "Most Occidental people do so for psychological reasons, in order to cope with the pressures of life." His observation has often come back to me as a reminder of the natural character of such religions when stripped of their ritual embellishments.

Some faiths are more historical (or revelatory). Judaism naturally comes to mind. Judaism and Christianity enjoy a common line of descent from the fathers and through the prophets. Both have subsequently evolved, the former in connection with rabbinic teaching, and the latter as a messianic movement.

This brings to mind what struck me at the time as a rather

amusing, but no less provocative, incident. A petite rabbi stood shoulder to waist beside me. "Do you suppose," he speculated, "that when I say that the Messiah will come and you say that he will return, we are talking about the same event?" Perhaps so. He awaited a Messiah as yet to come, while I anticipated his return.

Islam also falls into the historical category but constitutes a very different kind of challenge for the Christian apologist. Muhammad had previous contact with both Jews and a deviant form of Christianity. He at first showed considerable deference to these "people of the Book," but became more strident when they failed to embrace his beliefs.

A Christian colleague and I sat together with four Muslims in one of their homes. Among them were a religious judge and a retired university professor. The professor spoke first: "Now, concerning the Trinity." I had anticipated that this topic would be up for conversation, but before I could speak he continued. "This ought not to concern us. While I can't accept the Christian dogma, the idea of complexity with reference to God constitutes no problem. Let us get on to something of more substance."

He turned quickly to the issue of turning the other cheek rather than retaliation. "We Muslims say, 'Hit him back.' It will be good for both of us." Such are the unexpected directions discussion can take among those of differing faiths.

There are countless other religions. Some are ethnic, others traditional, and still others cosmopolitan. A blending of beliefs abounds. The Christian apologist has to adapt to multiple variations of the themes advanced earlier.

On the other hand, the situation may not be as confusing as it would first appear. People are deep down much the same, regardless of religious affiliation. We have needs that we believe Jesus can profoundly meet. While it is legitimate to target our message, we ought not to overlook our human commonality.

Some years ago I was talking with an engaging young convert from Buddhism. "What approach would you suggest to someone of Buddhist persuasion?" I asked. "Much the same as you would use to anyone else," she replied. "The gospel has a unique appeal to people, regardless of their religious, ethnic, or social backgrounds." I concluded that she was wise beyond her years.

While religions abound, there is only one true faith—Christianity. In this chapter I have tried to show the relationship of these other religions to the Christian faith. In so doing, we have presented corollary evidence in our developing case for Christianity. As we turn to the concluding chapter, we will consider, in light of the evidence we have presented, the question of Christianity's credibility.

DISCUSSION QUESTIONS

1. Review Anderson's approaches to world religions. Which do you think most pertinent to bear in mind for apologetic purposes?

2. Is some combination of the approaches more likely than one in particular? Why or why not?

3. As we look at other religions, what might we hold in common with them, from an apologetic standpoint? How is our faith distinct from them?

4. Why is it important, for apologetic purposes, to keep foremost in our thinking our common humanity, rather than being swept away by real or imagined differences? Illustrate from your experience.

CHAPTER 13

Is Christianity Credible?

WE have not reached the end, but the beginning of the end with the searching question: "Is Christianity credible?" Is Christianity believable? Many have so concluded for nearly two thousand years. Others have doubted; some have not even taken the possibility seriously.

The issue is, nevertheless, urgent. If in fact we have entered the messianic era, the stakes have risen immeasurably. God's redemptive activity is straining toward a climax. We can either go with or struggle against the current, but we cannot expect to prevail against God. Our eternal destiny lies in the balance.

CRITERIA

C. Stephen Evans offers four philosophic criteria to establish the credibility of a religious faith: logical consistency, coherence, factual adequacy, and intellectual fertility.[1]

First, a religious system ought to observe the law of noncontradiction. It should be logically consistent with itself.

My favorite figure in the old *Star Trek* series was Mr. Spock. For him, things had to be logical. When others complained, he took it as a compliment. There ought to be something of Spock in all of us.

Supposed contradictions within Christianity tend to disappear upon closer scrutiny. Divine sovereignty and human freedom serve as a case in point. Peter finds no difficulty weaving the two themes together in his Pentecost address. Whereupon, he concludes: "So let it be clearly known by everyone in Israel that God has made this Jesus whom you crucified to be both Lord and Messiah!" (Acts 2:36).

As another noncontradiction, there is nothing inconsistent with regard to God's love and wrath. His love is unconditional and unrelenting, so that he will not settle for what sells us short. C. S. Lewis further describes hell as the last place prepared by a loving God for those who will accept nothing better from him.

A faith could avoid contradiction and still not pass the test of coherency. Evans aptly comments: "Coherence is a positive harmony, a fitting together of beliefs into an organic whole."[2] It requires that we fashion a convincing worldview.

Christianity has an enviable track record when it comes to constructing and maintaining its worldview. It has made this a high priority, seldom, if ever, consistently matched by its religious rivals. Critics have been prone to admit this fact, sometimes overtly, but more often by skirting the issue.

A credible religious faith should be willing and able to boldly enter the intellectual arena. Christian martyrs bettered their rivals in death; apologists must better their rivals in life. Christians feel constrained to contend for truth, confident that all truth is God's truth—as part of a coherent worldview.

Evans selects factual adequacy as his third criterion. Does the Christian faith account for all pertinent facts? Or does it achieve a high degree of internal consistency and more modest success with coherency by simply limiting the data? The first two questions can be misleading unless we include the third.

Christianity has not been inclined to back off from asking the hard questions. We observed how C. S. Lewis insisted on giving suffering its worst possible scenario, as if a welcomed challenge to faith. He perhaps intended to encourage us that we have nothing to fear but fear itself.

The discussion of religious pluralism was another example of exploring related matters. One might ignore rival faiths by limiting our attention to Christian evidences. We could do so, but not without raising doubts concerning the credibility of Christianity. No relevant data should be overlooked.

Intellectual fertility provides the final criteria. A credible faith ought not simply to give an orderly account of what is known, but introduce fresh insights. It should provide significant potential for growth.

We actually need to strike a balance in this connection. While it is important to break new ground, a credible faith should be able to conserve what is of value from the past. Creativity and conservation ought to exist in a constructive tension for best results. Christianity, at its best, has approximated this elusive ideal.

Albert Einstein observed: "Science without religion is lame, religion without science is blind."[3] Faith ought to cultivate further exploration and act to curb pride in our limited success.

Evans subsequently sums up: "A reasonable interpretation is one which accounts for the facts, suggests new insights, illuminates meaningful patterns and does so better than its rivals."[4] Christianity's credentials are passed on, not on the basis of subjective preference, past associations, or arbitrary selection, but by demonstrated criteria that have passed the rigorous test of critical dialogue.

Cumulative Evidence and the "Leap" of Faith

Cumulative evidence plays an important role in establishing a claim of any sort. Someone is not feeling well and visits his or her doctor. The physician prescribes an extensive battery of tests. He does not think that any single test will yield sufficient information on which to render an accurate prognosis. Thus, he advocates cumulative evidence.

Someone is charged with a serious crime. The prosecutor gathers all the evidence available to win a conviction. The public defender likewise collects evidence in order to win an acquittal. Both defer to cumulative evidence aptly presented.

Religious verification proceeds along a similar line. Evans appropriately elaborates:

> Thus the theist finds it strange that there should be a contingent universe, and wonders why it exists. He finds it stranger still that the universe should show abundant examples of beneficial order, and that it should seem to contain a moral as well as a physical order. When he adds to these considerations the mass of religious experiences in which people claim to be aware of God, theism becomes at the very least a plausible hypothesis, a reasonable interpretation of experience. Confronted by a well-attested special revelation, which was accompanied by miracles and which provides insight into his own life, giving him a deep understanding of his basic failure and genuine needs, such a person might very reasonably become an adherent of a living religion.[5]

Cumulative evidence, carefully explored, has brought him to the threshold of faith.

The "leap" of faith is perhaps an unfortunate metaphor. It would seem to imply a blind plunge into the unknown. Faith resembles more of a calculated trust. When enough substantial evidence has been accumulated, an appropriate decision seems called for.

The relationship between reason and faith, nonetheless, remains a complex one. Thomas Aquinas held that reason was endowed to humans at creation and is meant to assist them in the quest of a credible faith. While Aquinas admitted limits to reason, he held that it could demonstrate the existence of God and the human soul. It could also reveal the natural law, establish the divine origin and authority of the Roman Catholic church, illustrate the teachings of Scripture, and refute the arguments set forth against the Christian faith. We know in order to believe.

Blaise Pascal (1623–1662) came at the reason-faith relationship from the opposite perspective. He was one of the greatest geniuses France and the world has ever known. Vexed by the problems of getting around Paris, he invented a public transportation system. His provocative work *Pensées* (Thoughts) was a collection of ideas jotted down on whatever he happened to be thinking about at the time. He was a mathematician, scientist, man of letters, linguist, exegete, pious mystic, and apologist.

Pascal held that faith is a gift of God and a function of the heart. The heart has reasons unknown to reason. It senses God's presence; it responds to God's initiatives; most important, it responds to Christ. Pascal concluded that Christ is ultimately the proof of Christianity, to be appropriated by faith. We believe in order to know.

Reason and faith are, in fact, elements in a triad that includes revelation. Augustine held that all truth is, by nature, illumination. God is the sun of the soul. The latter sees because the former enlightens it. The Logos illumines every man born into the world (John 1:9).

Humans are, nonetheless, seriously inhibited in their quest for truth. They cannot cope with the vast information concerning the universe. Even if they could, they would lack the ability to properly interpret the data. More critical still, sin darkens our minds and alienates us from truth.

Revelation enters in at this critical juncture. We hear the truth claims of Christianity, carefully examine them, and reach an appropriate conclusion. Finally, we exercise faith in accordance with our findings and in response to divine revelation.

Christian faith, as bears repeating, is less a belief in something than in Someone. We may illustrate this by trusting our weight to a chair, but the analogy is weak—God does not resemble a chair. Christian faith more nearly resembles an unconditional confidence we put in another person. We are moved to affirm: "I would trust my life to him." That is precisely what we do when we exercise Christian faith: We trust our lives to the God who has revealed himself through the prophets and in Christ.

BLESSED ASSURANCE

Fanny Crosby enthusiastically wrote the lyrics:

> *Blessed assurance, Jesus is mine!*
> *O what a foretaste of glory divine!*
> *Heir of salvation, purchase of God,*
> *born of his Spirit, washed in his blood.*

Was her assurance called for? Should she or anyone else be so confident?

Some activity requires that it be done in a wholehearted fashion. Marriage serves as a case in point. The man and the woman must decide on the basis of evidence available to them whether a proposed union is desirable. Their confidence may be well placed or it may not. They have to make a decision. A tentative commitment would be tantamount to refusal.

Religious faith is similar in design. One has to reach a decision on the basis of cumulative evidence. This does not, however, rule out the possibility of subsequent reconsideration.

What one hopes for in marriage or in religious commitment is that the wisdom of the decision will be justified. Such may be the nature of the confidence expressed by Paul: "And we know that God causes everything to work together for the good of those who love God and are called according to his purpose for them" (Romans 8:28). He had put God to the test on countless occasions and found that his faith was not wanting.

One must act as if married in order to experience the rewards of marriage. So it is with religious commitment. One deliberately and enthusiastically enters into the relationship in order to benefit from it. Crosby was decidedly on target!

It may, nevertheless, be helpful to distinguish between logical and existential doubt. Logical doubt amounts to the willingness to entertain new evidence and compare it with previous information. The unwillingness to do so is more likely the result of credulity than genuine faith. We have our mind made up and want to keep it that way. Conversely, faith operates in the real world, where challenges to its credibility occur on a regular basis. Logical doubt is user friendly to a life of faith.

I have from time to time been criticized for being actively involved in interfaith dialogue. I maintain that genuine dialogue reflects not a lack of conviction, but strength. A faith that shies from encounter suggests a critical uncertainty.

Existential doubt is a persisting feeling that our religious confidence may, in fact, be invalid. While it is normal for some existential doubt to accompany faith, if it becomes too frequent or too great, it should be taken as a warning sign. If preventive measures are not taken, one's faith may be crippled or collapse altogether. Faith can tolerate only a limited amount of existential doubt. Once again, Crosby was on target!

We do not have the choice between faith and unbelief. We can only choose between rival faiths. Such arguments as may be leveled against faith, as such, cut all ways. We are all entered on the same course: to discover a credible faith.

Is Christianity credible? Eminently so! Our chapters have carefully laid out the apologetic evidence. There is a case to be made for Christianity. It passes the philosophic criteria with highest honors; it focuses on the incomparable figure of Jesus; it draws credibility from accumulative evidence; and it satisfies the conditions of trust. We need not, and ought not, settle for less!

DISCUSSION QUESTIONS

1. Review the criteria for establishing religious credibility. Do you sense that Christianity has better grades in one area than others? What implications can you draw?

2. In what ways does Christian faith resemble sitting on a chair, confidence in another person, and marriage? What other analogies can you offer?

3. How does reference to the "leap" of faith prove misleading? What alternatives can you suggest?

4. Review the triad of reason, faith, and revelation. What problems result with an emphasis on one to the exclusion of the others? Illustrate.

5. Reflect on Hebrews 11 concerning insights on faith. What do you discover? Discuss your findings with others.

NOTES

INTRODUCTION
1. William Dyrness, *Christian Apologetics in a World Community* (Downers Grove, Ill.: InterVarsity, 1983).

CHAPTER 1
1. Warren Young, *A Christian Approach to Philosophy* (Grand Rapids: Baker, 1960), 47–58.
2. Ibid., 55–57.
3. Thomas Kuhn, *The Structure of Scientific Revolutions* (Chicago: University of Chicago Press, 1970).
4. Young, *A Christian Approach to Philosophy*, 57.

CHAPTER 2
1. William James, *The Varieties of Religious Experience* (New York: Modern Library, 1902).
2. Horace Bushnell, *Christian Nurture* (1861; reprint, Grand Rapids: Baker, 1979).
3. Sven Norberg, *Varieties of Christian Experience* (Minneapolis: Augsburg, 1937).
4. Sigmund Freud, *The Future of an Illusion* (Garden City, N.Y.: Doubleday, 1964), 22.

5. Emile Durkheim, *The Elementary Forms of Religious Life* (New York: Free Press, 1956).
6. C. Stephen Evans, *Philosophy of Religion* (Downers Grove, Ill.: InterVarsity, 1982), 93.
7. C. S. Lewis, *The Problem of Pain* (New York: Macmillan, 1962), 16–18.
8. Evans, *Philosophy of Religion,* 93–94.
9. Ibid., 94.
10. Ibid., 95.

CHAPTER 3
1. Justin Martyr, *Dialogue with Trypho,* 8.
2. Justin Martyr, *First Apology,* 3.
3. Justin Martyr, *Dialogue with Trypho,* 45.
4. Tertullian, *The Apology,* 39.
5. Tertullian, *The Prescription against Heretics,* 7.

CHAPTER 4
1. Peter Berger and Thomas Luckmann, *The Social Construction of Reality* (Garden City, N.Y.: Doubleday, 1967), 94–96.
2. Ibid., 96.
3. Thomas Aquinas, *Summa Contra Gentiles,* 1.3.
4. J. W. S. Reid, *Christian Apologetics* (Grand Rapids: Eerdmans, 1969), 127.
5. Quoted in Reid, *Christian Apologetics,* 149.
6. Reid, *Christian Apologetics,* 167.
7. Audiotape of debate between J. Edwin Orr and Michael Scriven, n.d.
8. Bernard Ramm, *The Christian View of Science and Scripture* (Grand Rapids: Eerdmans, 1954), 43.
9. Ibid., 238.
10. Harvey Cox, *The Secular City: Secularization and*

Urbanization in Theological Perspective (New York: Macmillan, 1965).

11. Harvey Cox, *The Feast of Fools* (New York: Harper & Row, 1970).

CHAPTER 5

1. John Hick, *Philosophy of Religion* (Englewood Cliffs, N.J.: Prentice-Hall, 1973), 24.
2. Evans, *Philosophy of Religion,* 75.
3. Ibid.
4. Kelly James Clark, *Return to Reason* (Grand Rapids: Eerdmans, 1990), 54.
5. Aquinas, *Summa Contra Gentiles,* 1.4.

CHAPTER 6

1. C. S. Lewis, *The Problem of Pain* (New York: Macmillan, 1962).
2. Morris Inch, *My Servant Job* (Grand Rapids: Baker, 1979), 9.
3. Helmut Thielicke, *I Believe* (Philadelphia: Fortress, 1974), 23–24.
4. Jim Bishop, *The Day Christ Died* (New York: Harper, 1957).

CHAPTER 7

1. Victor Frankl, *Man's Search for Meaning* (Boston: Beacon, 1974).
2. Eugene Nida, *Religions Across Culture* (New York: Harper & Row, 1968).
3. John Warwick Montgomery, *Where is History Going?* (Grand Rapids: Zondervan, 1969).

CHAPTER 8

1. Warren Young, *A Christian Approach to Philosophy*, 48.
2. Plato, *Phaedo*, 79.
3. C. S. Lewis, *Mere Christianity* (New York: Macmillan, 1952).
4. Krister Stendahl, "Immortality of the Soul or Resurrection of the Dead" in *Immortality and Resurrection* (New York: Macmillan, 1965), 18.
5. Ibid., 19.
6. Ibid., 20.
7. Ibid., 46.

CHAPTER 9

1. Chaim Potok, *Davita's Harp* (New York: Fawcett Crest, 1985), 159.
2. Ethelbert Stauffer, *Jesus and His Story* (New York: Knopf, 1960), 194–95.
3. John Reumann, preface to Joachim Jeremias, *The Problem of the Historical Jesus* (Philadelphia: Fortress, 1964), vi.
4. Ernest Renan, *Life of Jesus* (New York: Modern Library, 1927), 185.
5. Ibid., 392.
6. Rudolph Bultmann, *Jesus and the Word* (New York: Scribners, 1958), 211.
7. Gunther Bornkamm, *Jesus of Nazareth* (New York: Harper & Row, 1960), 52.

CHAPTER 10

1. William Albright, *The Archaeology of Palestine* (Middlesex, U.K.: Pelican, 1960), 127–28.
2. John Warwick Montgomery, *History and Christianity* (Downers Grove, Ill.: InterVarsity, 1971), 29.

CHAPTER 11

1. David Hume, "Of Miracles," in *An Enquiry Concerning Human Understanding* (Indianapolis: Hackett, 1977), 97.
2. A. Berkeley Mickelsen, *Interpreting the Bible* (Grand Rapids: Eerdmans, 1963).
3. Josh McDowell, *Evidence That Demands a Verdict* (San Bernardino, Calif.: Campus Crusade for Christ, 1972), 174.
4. Morris Inch, *Understanding Bible Prophecy* (New York: Harper & Row, 1977), 1.
5. Bernard Ramm, *Protestant Christian Evidences* (Chicago: Moody, 1953).

CHAPTER 12

1. Norman Anderson, *The World's Religions* (Grand Rapids: Eerdmans, 1977), 231–32.
2. Thomas Owen, *Attitudes Toward Other Religions* (New York: Harper & Row, 1969).

CHAPTER 13

1. Evans, *Philosophy of Religion,* 169.
2. Ibid.
3. Albert Einstein, *Out of My Later Years* (New York: Macmillan, 1978), 26.
4. Evans, *Philosophy of Religion,* 169.
5. Ibid., 170.

SELECTED ANNOTATED
BIBLIOGRAPHY

Several works are listed below to assist the reader in expanding his or her familiarity with Christian apologetics, first through the texts themselves and then with help of their representative bibliographies.

Bush, L. Russ, ed. *Classical Readings in Christian Apologetics:* A.D. 100–1800. Grand Rapids: Zondervan, 1983. For those who would like a good introduction to primary resource material.

Dyrness, William A. *Christian Apologetics in a World Community.* Downers Grove, Ill.: InterVarsity, 1983. Dyrness uses to good advantage his experience in non-Western culture.

Dulles, Avery. *A History of Apologetics.* New York: Corpos, 1971. This is a well-crafted Roman Catholic exposition.

Lewis, C. S. *Mere Christianity.* New York: Macmillan, 1952. Of his several provocative works on Christian apologetics, this appears most basic.

Ramm, Bernard. *Protestant Christian Evidences.* Chicago: Moody, 1953. Ramm provides a succinct summary of some of the best in evidential literature.

———. *Varieties of Christian Apologetics.* Grand Rapids: Baker, 1976. This is a helpful treatment of apologetic systems, accenting subjective immediacy, natural theology, and revelation.

Reid, J. W. S. *Christian Apologetics*. Grand Rapids: Eerdmans, 1969. Reid's work is comparable to that of Dulles, but from a Protestant perspective.